I started to plod down th
Sonia was waiting for me.
fake smile as Chris would h

'You've got something f
'Four pounds is a lot for me to pay every week.'
'But you can afford it.' She spat the words at me,
her eyes like daggers.
So I got out four one-pound coins. She grabbed
them out of my hand . . .

Also available by Pete Johnson, and
published by Corgi Yearling Books:

THE CREEPER
*Winner of the 2001 Stockton Children's Book of the Year
Award*
*Pick of the Year, The Federation of Children's Book Groups
Book of the Year Award — Shorter Novel 2000*

EYES OF THE ALIEN
'Very readable and skilfully plotted'
OBSERVER

THE FRIGHTENERS
'Prepare to be thoroughly spooked'
DAILY MAIL
'Fine, clear writing, convincingly charts the troubled
friendship between a girl and a boy'
IRISH TIMES

THE GHOST DOG
*Winner of the 1997 Young Telegraph/
Fully Booked Award*
'Incredibly enjoyable'
BOOKS FOR KEEPS

MY FRIEND'S A WEREWOLF
'Will make any reader stop and think'
SCHOOL LIBRARIAN
A 1998 Book Trust Selection

THE PHANTOM THIEF
'Another fine book from Pete Johnson'
SCHOOL LIBRARIAN

RESCUING DAD
'Funny and light, but the humour disguises real
emotional truth and depth'
GUARDIAN

PETE JOHNSON

Traitor

Illustrated by
David Wyatt

CORGI YEARLING BOOKS

TRAITOR
A CORGI YEARLING BOOK : 0 440 86438 0

First publication in Great Britain

PRINTING HISTORY
Corgi Yearling edition published 2002

3 5 7 9 10 8 6 4 2

Set in Perpetua/Gill Sans by
Falcon Oast Graphic Art Ltd.

Corgi Yearling Books are published by Random House Children's Books,
61–63 Uxbr idge Road, London W5 5SA,
a division of The Random House Group Ltd,
in Australia by Random House Australia (Pty) Ltd,
20 Alfred Street, Milsons Point, Sydney, NSW 2061, Australia,
in New Zealand by Random House New Zealand Ltd,
18 Poland Road, Glenfield, Auckland 10, New Zealand
and in South Africa by Random House (Pty) Ltd,
Endulini, 5a Jubilee Road, Parktown 2193, South Africa.

Made and printed in Great Britain by
Cox & Wyman Ltd, Reading, Berkshire.

*Dedicated to the memory of
Dodie Smith — a constant
source of inspiration, on and
off the page.*

CHAPTER ONE
by Tom

'Tom.'

Someone was whispering my name.

Someone I couldn't see.

'Tom.'

There it was again. A girl's voice, too.

I strained my eyes.

I still couldn't see anyone.

'What do you want?' I called back.

The overhanging trees creaking and sighing in the wind were my only answer.

Someone obviously thought they were being funny. Well, I wasn't laughing.

I turned round. I was on my way home. My house is at the end of this narrow, twisty laneway which I'm not keen on walking down, especially when I'm late. Like tonight. Still, I'd soon be there now.

'You're late tonight, Tom. Been to football training, have you?'

I whirled round.

'Who is that?' I cried.

There was a weird kind of rattling sound. And then I was able to make out someone. A long dark figure. I could see the shadow of a hood too. It was just as if the Grim Reaper was calling me.

A cold chill ran over my body.

And then the figure moved towards me but very slowly, just as if it were walking on stilts. And yes, it was a girl, but dressed from head to toe in black – a girl who I was sure I'd never in my life seen before.

'Hello Tom,' she said.

'How do you know my name?'

'I know a lot about you.'

'Do you?' I faltered.

'Well, I should do. I've been watching you for weeks now.'

'And why have you been doing that?' I couldn't stop my voice from going all squeaky.

She moved closer to me: in that same slow, confident way. Now she was standing just under the orange street light.

And not only was she dressed all in black but she was wearing black lipstick and black eye-liner. Her face, though, was covered in white powder giving her a weird, half-dead look. And every time she moved she clattered and jangled because she was wearing so much jewellery.

She was kind of fascinating in a warped kind of way. But there was something odd and scary about her too. And why was a girl, who must be at least fifteen, so interested in a smallish eleven-year-old boy like me?

'You don't go to my school, do you?' I asked.

This was clearly the wrong thing to say, as her small, dark eyes immediately tightened. 'Oh no, the school I go to is a dump, not like yours. You go to the posh school.'

'Oh it's not—' I began.

'Yes it is,' she cut in sharply.

Well, I wasn't going to start an argument with her about it. But my school really wasn't posh. It was pretty small though, and you had to pass this exam if you wanted to go there. And by the most amazing fluke of the century I'd done just that.

I decided to end this convo now. She was

obviously a bit of a weirdo and the less I had to do with her the better.

'Afraid I've got to go now . . . er . . . ' I struggled to remember her name. Then I realized she hadn't told me it.

And she said, 'Oh, I'm sorry, where're my manners. My name is Chris.'

'Oh right, great.' I tried to smile up at her. 'Well, goodbye Chris.'

'Just before you go –' she lowered her voice confidingly. 'The thing is, I need to borrow some money from you, Tom.'

I started.

'It's only four pounds which is nothing to you. You can easily afford that.'

Actually, I couldn't. So I said firmly, 'Sorry, I haven't got any spare cash at the moment.' Then I said, 'Sorry,' again and decided to make a run for it.

I bolted forward and let out a gasp of horror. From the other direction two other hooded figures loomed up.

'I've just asked Tom if I could borrow some money,' Chris called across to them. 'But I'm afraid he wasn't very helpful. You'll just have to search him, Sonia.'

The taller of the two girls – and she was

massively tall — immediately began rifling through my pockets. Before I could even protest she'd found my wallet.

She held it in the air like a triumphant magician. 'No, that's mine,' I cried.

But she was already opening it. 'You little liar,' she shouted. 'You've got five pounds and forty pence on you. But we'll only take four pounds as we're not like boys. We're not greedy. Now raise your hands while I see what else you've got. Come on, hurry up.'

I did what she said. She began to frisk me and acted as if she had a perfect right to do it too. I was boiling over with anger and frustration.

And then she quickly discovered my mobile phone. Now, I'd only had it a week, as it had taken me ages to persuade Dad to get me one. And just today I'd gone round my class getting everyone else's mobile numbers to put on it.

'Don't touch that. It's brand new,' I blurted out. 'It cost over seventy pounds and my dad'll go mad if—'

But I wasn't able to say any more as Sonia had grabbed my tie and was pulling it round my neck as she hissed furiously in my ear, 'Don't you ever talk to us like that. You show us respect. Respect! Do you understand?'

She was yanking my tie so tightly it was really hard to speak. I had to drag the words out of the back of my throat. 'Yes. I'm sorry.'

Sonia's eyes were still burning with rage. But then Chris said quietly, 'All right, he won't let his mouth run off like that again. He knows how he should speak to us now.'

Sonia whacked me another furious glare, then let go. My head swimming, I sagged back. In fact, I just stopped myself from falling over. Then I started to cough.

For ages I couldn't stop. Not only because of the way Sonia had been gripping my tie, but also because she was wearing a really strong perfume.

The three of them stood watching me cough my guts up as if I were some strange creature they'd discovered in an alleyway. They were sort of interested, but not at all concerned. In Sonia's eyes there was still a glint of anger too.

Finally, I stopped. And Chris said, 'Now, we're going to borrow your mobile phone.'

'To teach you some manners,' cut in Sonia.

'And we'll be back to collect another four pounds next week,' went on Chris.

'What!' I exclaimed.

'Just look on it as your going-home tax,' called out the girl who'd arrived with Sonia. She was dressed just like the others only her hair was streaked with green and red. This was the first thing she'd said. Sonia and Chris laughed at her comment. She grinned with pride.

Then Chris leant down and put her face right up close to mine. I began to cough. She was wearing the same perfume as Sonia. In a voice so quiet it sent shivers down my spine, she whispered, 'Whatever you do, don't grass us up. Remember, we know where you live.'

CHAPTER TWO
by Tom

Why had those girls singled me out?

Just as lions pick out the weakest animal in the herd, had they watched me roaming about the village and thought: now he's a right soft touch?

I can see why they might have thought that. I'm fair-haired and so small and skinny you can see my ribs. I couldn't even fight the tide in my bath. I'm not tough or hard at all. But — and this is the total truth now — I've never been picked on in my life before.

Well, except once when a boy stuck a pencil in my leg. But he was a bit of a headcase and did mad things to everyone, including the teachers.

But other than that no-one's ever bullied me. The reason is quite simple: I make people laugh. I'm quick-witted and act daft in class. And that has – until now – masked the fact that I'm not exactly big.

Anyway, that night, I sat in my bedroom just thinking and thinking about what had happened. How long had those girls been watching me? What else did they know about me? I got myself all worked up and worried. And I just knew I had to talk to someone else about this. But who?

I live in a village miles away from my school. And only two other people from my class hang out here.

Oliver is a swot. A real teacher's pet. And I couldn't imagine myself having a convo with him about anything.

Mia's all right, though. I like her. And we have a bit of a laugh on the bus sometimes. But could I tell her about today? No way. It's far too shaming and embarrassing to talk to a girl about.

Still, I could always phone a mate. Just one problem with that. Although I've got lots of friends, I don't know if I could trust any of them to keep today's humiliating incident to themselves. And if that got round the school . . . well, I'd look a right weakling, wouldn't I?

I could hear their comments already. *'Poor little Tom picked on by girls, were you?'*

I'd lose all my respect in one day.

So that just left my dad. When he got home I went down to say hello. My mum died when I was two and unfortunately I don't remember her at all. Then for yonks and yonks it was just Dad and me until he acquired a 'lady-friend'.

It didn't bother me at first as I hardly saw her. Then Dad announced she was coming to 'share Christmas with us'.

And on Christmas Day when we were tucking into the biggest turkey you've ever seen, Dad started flashing this engagement ring about. Put me right off my food, I can tell you.

She and Dad have been married for nearly three months now. And she's not horrible to me. In fact, she's all right, even told me to call her Lydia (which I do).

But she doesn't like this house much or where we live. I know that because I've heard her on the phone to her friends in London moaning on and on about 'life in the sticks'. She also thinks Dad deserves a better job than he's got: says he's not appreciated enough. Goes on about that a lot.

Anyway, after tea Dad and Lydia sat on the couch holding hands. No, they haven't grown out of that yet. I sat there, feeling like a right gooseberry, until Dad suddenly realized I was in the room as well and asked, 'Everything all right, Tom? You seem a bit quiet tonight.'

So there it was, my cue to tell him. But then Dad went on, 'Oh yes, how did football training go?'

My dad was captain of his school rugby team and was pretty disappointed when I showed no talent for rugby at all.

Still, I built up some credit with him when I made the school football team. I ran all the way home to tell him and we went out for a pizza to celebrate. But all my credit was going to evaporate when he heard I was being terrorized by girls. And it made me appear so weak, didn't it? So I just told him about football practice instead. He liked that and by the time I'd finished he had a big smile on his face.

Then I went into the kitchen, dug out the Yellow Pages and rang up the college about karate classes. There weren't any vacancies now but the lady at the college was really friendly and took my name down and told me to ring again in January.

January. But that was two and a half months away!

And I saw that girl-gang the very next day.

I'd got off the bus home and gone into the café to get a cake when I spotted the three of them sitting around a table. Sonia was carving her name on the table with a knife. She was doing it quite openly. And no-one was stopping her. The flustered-looking girl behind the counter was just acting as if she couldn't see her.

I was about to leave (all my appetite for that cream cake had just vanished) when Chris leant forward and hissed at me, 'Monday.' At once, three pairs of eyes were boring into me. I fled.

By Monday I had a plan, though. I'd escape them by going the long way home. But when I got off the bus I saw the girl with the green and red hair streaks watching me. She had a mobile phone pinned to her ear (mine!). I knew then they'd anticipated me taking a different route. And if I did that they'd just follow me.

So I started to plod down the laneway as usual. And Sonia was waiting for me. She didn't even give me a fake smile as Chris would have done.

'You've got something for me,' she snapped.

'Four pounds is a lot for me to pay every week.'

'But you can afford it.' She spat the words at me, her eyes like daggers.

So I got out four one-pound coins. She grabbed them out of my hand.

'Next Monday another four pounds. Don't ever think of not paying,' she hissed.

I hated the idea of giving this lot money every week. But do you know, I hated having to see them every week even more. I think I'd rather have mailed the money to them. But I knew they'd never agree to that. Ambushing me every week was much more fun.

'My mobile phone,' I piped up. 'My dad's asked me about it . . .'

'Oh, has he?' There was real venom in her face now. 'Your dear daddy. Well don't you dare tell him anything, will you?'

'No, I won't,' I cried.

'And you might get your phone back when you've learnt some manners, then again you might not.'

Then she laughed out loud as if she'd made a joke — although it was more of a bark than a laugh.

And I crawled home.

CHAPTER THREE
by Mia

The bus home was wheezing along at two miles an hour and I was so bored.

The first bus I have to get – that's the one into town – isn't too bad. A lot of my class catch that one. But the second one back to my village just takes for ever.

Usually Tom's around and he's a good laugh but he had football training, so I sat on the top of the bus all by myself, sending text messages to girls at school. Dead exciting messages too like, 'Are you going to hand in your English homework tomorrow?'

Suddenly I remembered there was someone else I could talk to: Oliver. Now he always sat downstairs by himself – and I didn't really know him. He didn't go to my last school (went somewhere much grander) and in the few weeks I have known him – well, he's not made a great impression. In fact, everyone thinks he's a stuck-up snob, because he's got a posh voice, is very keen in lessons and brings his lunch to school in a Harrods bag (actually he only did that once).

He never stops talking to the teachers in lessons and hardly says a word to us out of them. At breaktime, sometimes I'll see him shuffle past all by himself. And no-one says a word to him; they just look through him as if he's not really there.

Poor Oliver. I'm sure he'd be glad of some company now. And I can ask him about that badge he wears all the time. It's dead unusual: there's a gold star in the middle of a white circle with a gold rim all around the edges.

I've often wondered if there's any special reason why he wears it every day. Someone did ask him once. But he totally clammed up, said, 'Sorry, I can't talk about that.' Still, maybe he'd tell me.

I was just getting up when I heard footsteps coming up the stairs. By a weird coincidence Oliver must have decided to visit me too.

But the person I saw wasn't Oliver.

It was a girl dressed all in black and covered in jewellery. I'd seen her hanging around the village with a couple of other older girls. She saw me, smiled, and then to my total amazement came and sat down next to me.

'You're Mia, aren't you?' she said.

'Yes, how do you know that?'

She gave a strange, tight smile. She had dark purple lips and a very thin face — like a snake's. 'I know all about you. Oh, where are my manners? My name is Chris.' She stared at me for a moment, gave that odd smile again and said, 'Your hair's very red. Do you dye it?'

'No, it's naturally ginger I'm afraid.'

'I bet you get lots of comments about it.' The girl shook her head at me. 'I'd really hate to have hair that red.'

Well, thanks so much for sharing that with me, I thought. But I didn't say anything. There was something about her, with her mock friendliness and cold, dark eyes which unnerved me. I wished she'd go away.

'You keep your uniform nice and neat,' she went on.

'Thanks.'

'How I wish I had a posh uniform like that.'

I wasn't sure what to say to that. I didn't even know if she was being serious, or making fun of me.

She continued. 'My school's excluded me and I don't think I'll ever go back. Not that I care. It's a total dump. Not like yours.' She leaned forward. 'That's such a nice bag you've got too. Did your mum buy it for you? I expect she did. My mum's out of work.' All at once she was staring right at me.

'Oh, I'm sorry,' I said quickly. 'My dad was made redundant from his job last year and he's only just got a new job. He started this week in fact and he's got to go on lots of courses to catch up . . .'

I stopped. It's hard chatting with someone whose face has as much expression on it as a block of wood. So I tried to turn away from her. And I wished the bus would hurry up. I even wondered about jumping off the bus early. Anything to get away from this weird girl.

But she was putting her face up to my ear now, just as if she were about to whisper a secret. 'The thing is, Mia,' she said, in a low, urgent voice, 'we need to borrow four pounds from you.'

At the same time I heard footsteps clattering up the stairs. Two other girls came jangling over to us. They stood over me like bodyguards.

One girl was very tall and fierce-looking, the other was much shorter with streaks in her hair. 'I've just been talking to my new friend, Mia,' said Chris. 'She's going to lend me four pounds and looking at her, I'd say she can afford that, wouldn't you?'

The two girls nodded solemnly. 'And we really don't want to have to search you,' said Chris in a very reasonable voice, the kind a policeman might use.

'But we will if we have to,' said the very tall girl.

'No, no, it's all right.' I could hear the panic rising in my voice. I fumbled about in my purse. 'Yes, here it is. You wanted to borrow four pounds, wasn't it?'

Chris snatched the money out of my hand, then closed her fist on it.

'Look on it as a permanent loan,' said the other girl. Chris and the tall girl both laughed at that. Then the tall girl seized hold of my bag and tipped all the contents onto the floor.

'What's she doing?' I cried.

'It's all right,' said Chris, in that reasonable voice again, 'Sonia's just very nosy ... best leave her to get on with it.'

Actually, there wasn't much of interest in my bag, mainly just school books and stuff. But snuggled underneath my jacket was my mobile phone. How long before they discovered that? Luckily there wasn't time, as the bus finally reached my village.

'Bye Mia,' called Chris. 'We'll be back for another four pounds next week.'

'But you can't,' I protested. 'I only get three pounds a week pocket money.'

Chris looked surprised. 'Really?'

'Yes, honestly. You see, my dad's been out of work for a year.'

'Well, look at it this way,' said Chris. 'My dad's never had a job at all. And I've got far more expenses than you.'

'But it's my money, not yours,' I replied, but only after they had gone.

I hastily scooped up all my things, scrambled downstairs and watched the three girls swaggering down the High Street together, really pleased with themselves.

I stood there, choking with anger. The whole thing had been planned, of course. That girl called Chris would come upstairs first, pretending to be all friendly with me. But really she was just like those cats who, before they kill their prey, fling it up and down and play with it for a bit. That's exactly what she'd been doing with me. Then she and the other girls had moved in and pounced.

Well, just who did those girls think they were? And did they really believe I'd meekly hand over another four pounds to them next week? They could whistle for it.

I felt quite brave now. But I knew it would be very different the next time they surrounded me again.

When I got home I hadn't meant to tell my mum anything. I'll tell you why.

Earlier this year Mum was rushed into hospital with a ruptured appendix. She's been very ill indeed. And even after she came out of hospital Aunt Carrie stayed with us.

In fact, Aunt Carrie only left about two weeks ago and Mum still has to take things very carefully. Just before he went off on his course yesterday Dad said in this very serious voice, 'You will keep an eye on your mum for me, won't you?' I said of course I would. He also told me to make sure Mum didn't lift anything heavy.

So that night I set the ironing board up for her and heaved my brothers, Russell and Martin (they're twins aged four), in and out of the bath. But all the time little flashes of what had happened on the bus kept jumping in and out of my head.

Still, I thought I'd hidden my feelings pretty well. But I hadn't because when I was sitting in bed, right out of the blue, Mum came and sat beside me and whispered, 'Come on, what's up, love?' She took me so completely by surprise I blabbed it all out.

Mum doesn't often get really mad (Dad's the one with the temper), but she did then.

'How dare those girls behave like that,' she cried. 'I know one of them, too.'

'Do you?'

'Well, I've heard about her. A friend of mine has the great misfortune to live near Christine Freyer and her sisters and her mother. They keep the neighbourhood awake with their loud music and their rows. And Christine is the worst of them. No, don't worry, love . . .'

'What are you going to do?' I asked anxiously.

'I shall ring up her school.'

'But she's been excluded, Mum.'

'Oh.' She looked taken aback for a moment. Then she put an arm around me and whispered, 'Don't worry. Just leave this to your mother to sort out.'

CHAPTER FOUR
by Mia

Next day at school I kept thinking about my mum and wondering what she was going to do. I should never have told her. She wasn't strong enough to deal with the likes of Christine Freyer. I imagined her having a row with Christine Freyer's mum and then collapsing with exhaustion.

I rang up my home a couple of times. No answer. That was unusual as my mum hadn't been going out much in the day.

Oh, I just couldn't wait to get back. The bus took for ever, as usual. But at least Tom was there to chat with.

And then those girls came clomping back on the bus again. The breath caught in my throat. I was sure they were going to come over. But instead, the three of them sat at the back, whispering and talking very loudly.

I kept sneaking looks at them. I noticed Tom giving them a quick, darting glance too. They were certainly being very loud. But at least they were ignoring me. Could that mean – my heart gave a little leap – my mum had actually scared them off? Oh, how wonderful if she had.

As the journey went on I became more and more hopeful. Good old Mum. She'd sorted them out for me all right. I was so glad I'd told her now.

I smiled at Tom.

'You look happy,' he grinned.

'I am.' In fact, I was so relieved I felt slightly sick if that makes sense.

The bus pulled into my stop. The three girls stormed down the steps. Tom and I followed. I noticed Oliver downstairs too. He'd been especially quiet and subdued today. So I smiled at him and was about to ask if he was all right when something truly awful happened.

This high, shrill voice called out, 'Christine Freyer, I want a word with you. And you other girls too.'

Do you know what my first thought was? I shall get back on the bus again and pretend that woman making a complete show of herself, and me, is not my mum.

And for a moment I was very, very tempted. But of course I didn't do that. I couldn't abandon Mum, even when she was being totally embarrassing.

Now she was shrieking, 'I've heard how you've been demanding money from my daughter here.' She pointed at me, while I hung my head. I just knew I was flushing bright red.

The three girls gathered around Mum. 'Is that what Mia told you?' demanded Chris contemptuously.

'Don't deny it,' shrilled Mum. 'I know everything that happened on the bus yesterday and it's got to stop.'

Standing just behind me now was Tom. Oliver

was hovering around too, while a small crowd had gathered for a gawp at the free show.

'At least hear our side of it,' purred Chris Freyer in that cool, reasonable voice of hers. The other two girls stood either side of her, as still as waxworks. And they didn't look bothered by Mum's accusations at all. I suddenly thought, if they're not afraid of people's parents, who are they scared of?

'Yes, we are friendly with Mia,' said Chris Freyer, smoothly. 'And yesterday she told us you only gave her three pounds a week pocket money. Is that true?'

'None of your business,' cried Mum, her voice getting higher-pitched every time she spoke.

'Well, Mia was moaning to us about only getting three pounds a week. That's why we said to her, why not tell your mum you've lent us some money then you might get some more.'

'That's a total lie.' The words tore out of my throat. And for a moment everyone started eyeballing me.

Chris gave a sharp, cold laugh. 'Oh Mia, you are being so naughty. I think you should just ask your mum for a rise in your pocket money. But please don't drag us into it. We can't help you any more.' Then the three girls linked arms.

'I believe my daughter, not the rubbish you've

been spouting,' shrieked Mum. The girls just laughed, then they began to march down the High Street together like a small, invading army.

I walked over to Mum. But a woman in black glasses who ran the newsagent's got to her first. 'I wouldn't believe a word those girls say,' she cried. 'Whenever I'm away they swarm into my shop causing chaos. Absolute chaos. When I question them afterwards, of course they deny everything. And my assistants are too scared of them to name names – but I know it's those girls . . .'

She and Mum went into a kind of huddle while I – well, I just didn't know what to do. Especially as people were still murmuring about what had happened and looking at me as if I were some kind of exhibit. No wonder my face was on fire. Then I heard a little breath behind me. I turned round.

It was Oliver. He spoke very slowly, as if every

word was an effort. 'I know you're telling the truth. They've taken money from me too.'

I was really shocked. I gaped at him.

'So I just wanted you to know, you're not the only one.'

Then Tom, who'd been listening to all this, took a couple of steps forward, just as if this was a games lesson and he'd been picked to be in my team.

'I'm in on this too,' he muttered.

Now I was totally stunned. 'You mean . . .'

He put up a hand. 'We can't talk about it here. It's best we meet somewhere in private like . . . well, I've got somewhere at my house where we won't be disturbed. Can you come around tonight after tea, say about seven o'clock?'

I nodded.

'Erm, excuse me, but did you want me to join you?' asked Oliver.

'Of course we do,' I said at once. 'Don't we, Tom?'

'OK. Why not?' he replied. 'See you both later then.'

'Just one point,' asked Oliver. 'Where exactly do you live?'

Tom gave Oliver his address and then I noticed my mum had vanished. I looked around and saw the woman from the newsagent's signalling me to come over. 'Nothing to worry about, dear, but your mum felt a bit faint so she's inside.'

I sped into the shop. Mum was sitting on a chair, sipping a glass of water. She looked deathly pale and there were tired lines around her eyes.

I crouched down beside her. Seeing my alarmed face, Mum smiled. 'No, I'm fine. I just felt a bit dizzy for a moment out there.'

But I hated seeing my mum like this again. She'd been doing so well lately too. Yet, now, it was as if she'd gone back several weeks. And all because of me pulling her into this.

On the way home Mum explained. 'I spoke to Christine Freyer's mother on the phone first. She was polite enough but said she was sure I'd made a mistake. Her daughter would never do anything like that. So I thought it would be best if I confronted the girl directly. I got Mrs Adams to look after the boys and . . . do you think I've helped at all?'

Helped!

Why, Mum hadn't even wounded them. All she'd done was stir them up even more.

Helped!

Actually, Mum had made everything much, much worse. I didn't tell her that, though. She'd done her best. But she just wasn't well enough to take them on at the moment.

'Oh yes, you really have,' I lied.

Mum looked pleased. 'Well, from now on I'll meet you off the bus every day.'

'What!' I cried.

'Don't worry, I'm sure Mrs Adams won't mind looking after . . .'

'Mum, if you do that I'll die.' My voice rose. 'I will. I'll die of shame.'

'Oh come on,' she protested.

'No, Mum, if you wait by the bus stop for me I'll look such a baby . . . please don't do that. Please!'

Mum was completely taken aback by my re-action. So I pressed on. 'Look, you've made your point. Those girls know you're watching them, but just leave it now, please.'

In the end Mum backed down — but not before she'd made me promise to tell her if Christine Freyer tried to take any more money from me.

Well, I made that promise all right. But I had my fingers crossed at the same time.

CHAPTER FIVE
by Tom

It was just something I never, ever expected to see.

A wet lettuce like Oliver turning up at my house.

It was really pretty freaky watching this big car pull up, and then seeing Oliver and his mum get out of it. For one awful moment I thought she was going to come in with him. But instead, she just planted this kiss on the top of his forehead (aaah) and then whizzed off.

He stood there waving away to her (aaah, again) and then slowly turned into my abode. He was about to ring on the doorbell when I opened the door. He sprang back in surprise and said, 'Oh, good evening.'

Those three words tell you all you need to know about Oliver. No-one of my age goes around saying 'Oh, good evening'. It's practically illegal, isn't it? But then Oliver is one of those people who were born aged forty-nine.

He's about my height but with a face that looks a couple of sizes too big for his body, if you know what I mean. He's got dark brown hair and very serious, very intense blue eyes.

Today, his face was also extremely red. I wasn't sure if he was very cold or just nervous. I also hadn't a clue what to say to him. So I was pretty relieved when Mia bowled up a few seconds later.

Oliver said 'Good evening' to her too and I noticed her lips twitching a bit.

'Right, follow me, folks,' I said.

'Where are we going?' asked Oliver.

'To my office,' I replied. That puzzled Oliver even more. I opened the back gate. He and Mia stared around at the long, narrow, overgrown garden in some bewilderment. Then Mia spotted it.

Tucked away behind the trees was a small, weatherbeaten shed with a sloping roof.

Mia smiled at me. 'That's your office, isn't it?'
I grinned back and nodded.

'And we're going inside there, are we?' asked Oliver.

I chuckled. 'We sure are, Oliver. And it really is all mine. It belonged to my dad first of all, but just before he got married again he gave it to me. So, come in.'

I opened the door and switched on the light.

'The first thing you will notice,' I said, 'is the smell. That's the timber roof. Then you will see the battered, old workbench.' I pointed. 'While over there is a CD player and a fairly pathetic number of CDs. And please don't miss the tiny windows which are permanently fogged over. But it has, in the corner, one of the world's finest collections of dead wasps.'

Mia grinned. 'I think it's so cool to have this. It's a bit like camping, isn't it?'

'Only tents don't have sofas in them. It's a pretty ancient sofa and a lot of the stuffing is coming out of it, but it is surprisingly comfortable. And as you're both my guests you can have the great honour of parking yourselves on it tonight.'

So Mia and Oliver both settled themselves on my green leather sofa. And Oliver's eyes kept widening with amazement. I don't think he'd ever seen anything quite like this shed before. He went to take his coat off.

'Actually, Oliver, you might want to keep your coat on. It's quite draughty at the moment.' Then I added, 'Now I'll tell you the really good thing about this shed. It's got a latch on the inside.' I got up and showed them. 'So no parents can barge in. We're totally private.'

I leant against the workbench. 'What we're about to discuss is for our ears only. Not anyone else's. All right?' I was beaming my gaze straight at Oliver now. He nodded. So did Mia.

I went on, 'So how about if we just say exactly what's happened to us.' They looked at me expectantly, thinking I was about to start. But I'm no fool. I was going to hear what they had to say before I told them a thing. 'How about if you start first, Oliver.'

'Yes, certainly.' He gave this massive gulp and then looked down at his shiny shoes. 'Two weeks ago I was coming home from school when this girl called out my name. When I turned round, three girls were standing behind me. They said they needed to borrow some money from me. When I said they couldn't they got angry . . . especially the very tall one.'

'Sonia,' I murmured.

'So then I saw my chance and ran away.'

'You ran,' I yelled, disbelievingly.

Oliver is not one of our school's great athletes. And the mind just boggled at the idea of him running anywhere. I noticed Mia smother a laugh. Luckily Oliver didn't notice. He just went on talking to his shoes.

'I thought I'd seen the last of them for that day. But later I looked out of my window and there they were.' His voice began to shake. 'Standing right outside my house. There were five of them.'

'Five,' Mia and I echoed together.

'Yes, the three girls I'd seen before and two others.'

So this girl-gang was bigger than we'd supposed. That was not good news. I wondered exactly how many there were in it.

'And all five of them were just standing there, looking at the house. It was horrible to see them staring in at us. I went round and drew all the curtains. But I could still hear them talking and laughing outside.' His lip quivered. 'I hated them knowing where I lived.'

And I understood exactly what he meant.

'Now, my mother was out but Nan was there. And I was especially worried about her, because last month some burglars broke into our house.

My nan heard them and very bravely crept down-stairs by herself. She saw two figures in the hallway. Then one of the figures knocked her down.'

'Was she all right?' asked Mia.

'Yes, thank you. The doctor said she's made a remarkable recovery for her age.' He said this proudly. 'But she still walks with a limp . . . and she doesn't like the dark any more. She can only get to sleep with the light on now, and she's still in an extremely nervous state. So the last thing I wanted was for her to see all those people outside our house. I just wished I could pick up my house and go somewhere else. But of course I couldn't do that. And as I'm the man of the house and the one the gang were pursuing, I went outside and . . . paid them the money.'

He paused and slowly looked up. 'They said they'd be back for more.'

'And have they?' I asked.

'Oh yes. I've seen them again.' Then he touched the badge which he always wore to school and, tonight, was pinned on his coat.

'Thanks for telling us all that, Oliver,' whispered Mia. Then she recounted everything that had happened to her. After which it was my turn.

I coughed, cleared my throat twice and ended up telling them the whole lot. I don't think I missed out a single detail.

'I hate them,' cried Mia, after I'd finished. 'I really, really hate them.'

'One thing to remember, though,' began Oliver.

'Yes,' said Mia, encouragingly.

'Well, I was picked on quite badly at my old school too. And one day someone threw my bag out of the window, which was somewhat frustrating.'

I smothered a smile. I couldn't look at Mia.

'But then Mummy said . . .'

Mummy!

'That when people pick on you, don't take it personally. They're really doing it because they don't like themselves and . . .'

'Right, thanks for that, Oliver. Next time the gang are stealing money off me I'll remember that and feel so much better,' I said, dead sarcastically.

'But the big question is — what are we going to do about them? As I see it, we've got three options. The first is to try and fight them back.'

'Oh, very ill-advised,' said Oliver at once. 'Mummy says violence always breeds more violence.'

'Your mummy says a lot, doesn't she?' I replied.

Oliver lowered his head, like a tortoise going back into his shell . . . while Mia gave me a stop-being-so-snidey-to-Oliver look.

'I can do karate,' I announced.

'Can you?' asked Mia.

'Well, not yet. But I will be able to, soon. I'm starting classes in a few weeks. So then I'll be able to scare that gang bloodless.'

'But right now, we've got no chance,' said Mia.

'Agreed. So option two is we get the crinklies to do something.'

'Excuse me,' asked a puzzled-sounding Oliver, 'but who exactly are the crinklies?'

Mia giggled. 'Tom means our parents.'

'Oh, I see,' murmured Oliver.

Then Mia grew serious. 'Just before I came out I heard my mum calling the doctor and I'm sure what happened today didn't help her at all. So I can't involve her any more in this. As for my dad . . . well he's away at the moment, but we could keep him in reserve.'

'I'd say my dad's a reserve too,' I said. 'I'd rather not bring him in unless it's a real emergency.' I turned to Oliver. 'How about Mummy?'

'I'd like to solve this without involving her. I assume your third option is: we sort it out ourselves.'

'Well guessed, Oliver. They may be bigger and stronger than us, but I bet they're not as clever. After all, you two have got brains the size of planets.'

'I wish,' cried Mia.

'And I've got four swimming certificates,' I joked. They both laughed at that.

'So all we've got to do is frisk our brains a bit for a masterplan.'

Just saying masterplan really perked everyone up.

I went on, 'I also think we need to find out more about this girl-gang, especially as they know so much about us. So tomorrow night I'm going on a kind of mission behind enemy lines.'

'Sounds exciting,' said Mia.

I grinned. 'I'm going to find out exactly where this Christine Freyer lives – and the other two – and do a bit of detective work. The more we know about the enemy the better.'

'Do you want us to come too?' asked Mia.

'No, I think it might be better if this is Operation Solo. But I'll tell you what you can do.'

'Yes?' said Mia.

'My cover story to my dad and step-mum will be that I'm at your house tomorrow. So if they should ring, back me up, will you, Mia?'

'Of course I will and if there's anything else I can do just let me know.'

'I'm also keen to volunteer,' declared Oliver.

'Well, just keep thinking of a masterplan. That's your mission. Now, how about if we meet up here again in two days' time.'

They agreed.

'Just in case something happens before then, do you think we should exchange phone numbers?' asked Oliver.

So we did. Even though I cheerily said, 'After what happened with Mia's mum today I think they'll lie low for a few days.'

I was completely wrong.

CHAPTER SIX
by Mia

In fact, they struck the very next day.

And their target was – me.

It happened right after tea. Took me totally by surprise. And my stomach just turned over when I saw it. I fact, I was so horrified that I tore downstairs to tell my mum.

She was sprawled out on the settee, the news blaring out from the telly, fast asleep. I stood looking at her and kind of came to my senses. She was the very last person I should be telling.

I went back upstairs and started dialling Tom's number until I remembered he was out on his mission tonight. There was always Oliver. I hesitated. I hardly knew him really. But he was in on this and I had to tell someone.

He answered the phone and sounded quite pleased to hear my voice.

'Oliver,' I whispered. 'Can you come over right away?'

'Has something happened?' he asked.

'Yes.'

'Well, don't worry, I'll get Mummy to drive me round at once.'

Less than ten minutes later he arrived. I was waiting at the door for him.

I put a finger to my lips. 'Mum's asleep in there.' I nodded towards the sitting room. 'And I don't want to wake the twins either.'

We crept up the stairs to my room then I closed the door.

'Have you seen them again?' asked Oliver.

'Not exactly.' I picked up my mobile phone and pressed a button. 'You haven't got one of these, have you?'

'No, Mummy doesn't like them at all. She thinks they're very bad for your health and the level of communication on them is generally very poor . . . Why?'

'You can get text messages on them from friends. And today . . . today I got this.'

I handed him the mobile. And he read the words which I knew off by heart now: 2 MAMAS LTL GRL — YR MAMA CANT STAND 2 MCH STRS CN SHE? TKE BTR CARE OF HR IN FTRE OR ELSE C.I.S.

Oliver didn't say anything at first, just made this funny little noise in his throat. Then he patted his badge — which was on his coat, as usual — and looked at me. 'This is so . . .' his voice kind of cracked, 'so nasty.'

'I know.' My voice was cracking a bit too.

'Really, really nasty,' he went on, sounding both angry and amazed. 'And their spelling is just appalling.'

'No, that's the way lots of people write text messages now.'

'Oh I see,' he said in a puzzled voice. He sank down on my bed. Then he looked across at me. 'It must have been a horrible shock for you.'

'I totally freaked out at first. Ran downstairs to tell my mum. Luckily she was asleep and she looked so pale and ill.' A tear sneaked down my face. I hastily brushed it away. 'She isn't very strong at the moment.'

He nodded sympathetically.

I leaned forward. 'Oliver, when they wrote "take better care of her in future – or else", what exactly do you think they meant?'

Oliver considered. He looked just as if he were being asked to solve a particularly difficult mathematical problem. At last, he said, slowly, 'I think they're warning you not to involve your mother in this any more. They probably know you're worried about her and are using that to make sure you keep silent – and keep paying them, too. I think they're absolutely rotten,' he added.

The way he said 'rotten' made me want to smile.

But I didn't, because I knew he was being completely sincere.

'I was wondering,' he asked, 'how they knew what your mobile number was?'

'I'd been wondering that too. But they've got Tom's mobile, haven't they?'

He nodded.

'And Tom went round the class getting everyone's number.'

'So they've got it off that. And why are they signing themselves the C.I.S.?'

'Well, C is the first letter of Christine Freyer's name. S is the first letter of Sonia's. So maybe the other girl is called Ingrid or something, and they've put their first three letters together.'

'Sounds the kind of infantile thing they would do.' He shook his head, then stared around my bedroom. 'Oh my goodness,' he cried, suddenly.

'What!'

'You've got a television in your bedroom.'

He sounded as if this was something very unusual and exotic, when just about everyone I know has one.

'Why, so I have,' I teased. 'I never noticed it before.'

'I would like a personal television,' he said, unexpectedly, 'because, well they have some interesting programmes on – and good comedies too.'

'But your mum's not keen?'

'No, we have a television downstairs and I'm allowed to watch that occasionally. But Mummy thinks television is bad for your imagination and distracts you from your work and your hobbies.'

'Well, you can always come and watch mine.'

'Can I? Oh, thanks,' he said eagerly. 'That would be so fantastic.' He seemed really chuffed by my offer. He got up and went over to my dressing-table. Right in the centre was a little brown dog. He picked it up.

'This looks old.'

'I've had it since I was born, practically. It's my lucky mascot. And when I went into hospital to have my tonsils out last year, I had it by my bedside. It goes everywhere with me. And it's not at all valuable. But if my house was being burnt down and I could just rescue one thing, that's what it would be.'

I thought he might laugh at that. But he didn't. He just nodded and said, 'I had this little plastic turtle and when you pushed its tail it squeaked. I used to find that so hilarious and . . . I've still got it close by.'

We smiled at each other. And then my mobile phone let out a bleep.

'You've got another message,' whispered Oliver.

'This will be from a girl in my class . . .' I began, then stopped. It wasn't from a girl in my class. It was from them again. Just three words this time.

DONT 4GET MON

CHAPTER SEVEN
by Tom

'Look, we're going to win, remember that.'

It was the following night. We were in my shed. It was freezing cold and I thought Mia and Oliver needed a bit of a pep talk.

Mia was still upset about those two text messages from the C.I.S. – and I didn't blame her at all. They were also a bit depressed we hadn't thought of a masterplan yet.

'It will happen,' I said. 'Do not worry. Meanwhile, do you want to hear what I've got to report from last night's mission?'

'Of course we do,' cried Mia.

'Well, first off I found out where Christine Freyer lives: really run-down house it was too. Then I went into this little shop, down the road from her and guess who came in . . . only Christine Freyer's mum. And straightaway the woman behind the counter started having a go at her.

'Someone broke into her shop the night before and she thought it was Chris Freyer. But her mum – this small, very careworn-looking woman – sticks up for her daughter. She said Chris had been in with her all that night. She goes, "I'd stake my life on her innocence."

'This shut the woman behind the counter up. But I followed Chris Freyer's mum outside. And there she was, laughing with this other woman, saying, "The lies I've told for that girl."

'Then I went back into the shop and asked the woman in there about Christine Freyer. She told me masses. She said everyone hates the Freyer family and they've been trying to have them evicted for months. She also knew about Chris being in a gang. She said there were two other girls running it: Sonia and Itta. There are other girls as well who want to be in the gang, but have to prove their worth.'

'How many, exactly?' asked Oliver anxiously.

'She didn't say.'

He gulped. 'But are we talking five, ten?'

'She didn't say, Oliver. I reckon there's probably only about two or three of these wannabes.'

I rushed on. 'Anyway, the woman in the shop knew about Sonia too—'

'I really hate her,' interrupted Mia.

'I know, got the personality of a camel, hasn't she?' I said. 'I heard last night that Sonia also has a really bad temper. Mind you, I guessed that. She flips out at the slightest thing apparently. Been excluded from school for throwing chairs at people. And would you believe, she's got a boyfriend who's in prison.'

'I'd say he's had a lucky escape,' said Mia, dryly.

'She's also been chucked out of her house and has been staying with Chris Freyer for a while.'

'How cosy,' murmured Mia.

'As for the third girl: Streaky, I call her. But her real name is Itta. The woman in the shop knew about her too. She lives with her mum and stepdad in this white bungalow right on the corner. I was scrutinizing it when the door opened.'

'Was it her?' asked Mia.

'No, it was a man. Dead ugly. Looked just like a boiled egg before you crack the top. He glared at me and I glared at him – and then I came home.'

'You've found out masses,' said Mia.

I tried to look modest.

But what were we going to do about the C.I.S.?

That question hung in the air for the rest of the week. We met twice more, the second time on Sunday night. And the shed was warm now, thanks to the fan-heater donated by Oliver.

'I don't know what to say,' I said. 'Except, Oliver, you're a legend.'

But the atmosphere on Sunday night was pretty grim. Monday was fast approaching and there wasn't even a hint of a masterplan.

'My mind just isn't working properly,' sighed Oliver, tapping his badge as if he might get an idea from it.

'They've got us so rattled we can't think straight,' whispered Mia. 'Every time my mobile goes off I jump up thinking it's them again.'

'They haven't left any more poison messages, have they?' I asked.

'No, but I still keep expecting one.'

'Well, I have got one idea.'

They both looked at me eagerly.

'Now, it's not exactly a masterplan. It's just I've an uncle and aunt in London.'

'And so have I,' said Oliver. 'But sorry for the interruption.'

'That's quite all right. Anyway, their son, my cousin, is great. He's called Mick. He's fourteen and he's six foot already and I thought if I could get him and his mates to come down here one weekend and walk about with us – well, then the C.I.S. would see we've got some muscle behind us.'

Oliver looked distinctly unenthusiastic.

'It's only a thought,' I said. 'I haven't even spoken to Mick yet.'

'No, it's a good idea,' said Mia. 'It's just – well – what are we going to do when they come after us tomorrow?'

All at once she and Oliver were looking at me again.

'We're not going to pay them,' I said.

'Aren't we?' queried Oliver.

'No,' I replied, firmly. 'We're going to stand

up to them, stare them out if we have to. And what's more, we won't carry any money on us.'

'Oh that's a good idea,' cried Mia.

'Thanks, I've been saving that one up.' Actually I'd just thought of it. 'Because if we're not carrying any money – well what's the worst thing they can do to us?'

'Tip us upside down to check,' suggested Mia.

We all grinned at that.

'Won't we need some money for sweets, though?' asked Mia.

'Or emergencies,' cut in Oliver.

'OK, a pound for sweets or emergencies but that's all. Are we agreed?' Mia and Oliver nodded earnestly.

'Good.' I was really getting into my stride now. 'They'll probably strike after school. So Mia, I'll bodyguard you back to your house.'

'Oh, thanks Tom.'

'No problemo. If you come as well, Oliver, then I'll walk up to your house with you as well.'

Oliver looked so grateful I thought he was going to cry. 'But what about you?' he asked.

'Oh, I'll be all right,' I replied, carelessly. 'I think that gang is going to get a big shock tomorrow, because there's three of us working together now. And they don't know that.'

CHAPTER EIGHT
by Tom

On Monday morning the three of us met up at Mia's, as her house is between Oliver's and mine. And we strolled to the bus stop in pretty good spirits.

I remember Mia saying that if we put the first letter of each of our names together as the C.I.S. did, it spelt TOM. Hadn't noticed that before.

Of course it was just a laugh but I did feel as if I was their leader. And I knew they were thinking a lot about the C.I.S. (so was I) so I said we'd talk about the final details on the bus.

Then we went into the newsagent's to stock up

on our early morning supply of sweets — and walked straight into an ambush.

The moment I was in the shop I smelt their nasty horrible scent. I froze in horror. Then I heard a rattling, clanking sound. And there were all three of them, standing in a half-circle at the back.

Waiting for us.

Mia had gone charging down the shop to look at a magazine. She gave this panicky hiss. Sonia stared at Mia with a faintly amused smirk on her face, while Chris Freyer and the streaky-haired girl called Itta sauntered over to Oliver and me, both doing a slow, cocky walk as if they were the rulers of this whole village.

There was only one person serving: a boy who was hunched behind the counter and peering intently at his newspaper as if he found it dead fascinating.

Sonia grabbed a bar of chocolate, then bit off an enormous chunk. Bits sprayed out of her mouth as she hissed, 'Time to pay your tax.'

'And you'd better hurry up or you'll miss your bus and be late for school and that would never do, would it?' said Itta.

Mia looked around and then said softly. 'Sorry, but we haven't got any money on us.' She looked across at Oliver and me. 'Have we?'

'No, we haven't,' I said. Only my words were drowned out by the shop door opening. Two children from a different school to ours appeared.

Sonia tore down the shop in three strides. 'If you know what's good for you you'll get out of here now,' she snapped.

The children didn't stay and argue. I waited for the boy behind the counter to say something. But he didn't even seem to have noticed that anyone else was in his shop.

Sonia marched towards us again. 'Come on, hurry up.'

'But we told you,' cried Mia, in this tiny, desperate voice, 'we haven't any money on us.'

Chris looked at me. 'I do hope that's not true. As you can see, Sonia's not in the best of moods.' She leaned forward and whispered. 'Sonia hates early starts. And between you and me, when she's in one of her bad moods, well, she could do anything.'

Her voice was friendly but her eyes were small and completely expressionless. And I could feel those eyes sucking all the courage out of me.

'Have you got your tax, Tom?' asked Chris Freyer, coming even closer to me. Her scent was overpowering. And there was this awful heavy silence now, as if the whole shop was listening for my answer.

I opened my mouth to say, 'No, I haven't.' And the words were on my lips. Truly they were. But then Sonia moved nearer, gave me one of her death stares and the words died somewhere in my throat. And instead, I heard this shaking little jelly say, 'Yes, I have the money.'

I didn't look in my wallet but dug down into my right pocket. I drew out a five-pound note. And I was so deeply ashamed that I couldn't look at Mia at all. And then to make matters even worse, my right hand started to tremble.

I grabbed hold of my wrist with my other hand to try and steady it. But Chris Freyer saw and the corners of her lips began to twitch. Then she swiped the money. 'I'm sorry, but we don't give change.'

'Now your turn,' said Itta to Oliver. He looked as if he were in a dream, staring straight ahead and nodding his head very slightly, but he got out his wallet and handed Itta the money.

Sonia glared down at Mia, bristling with impatience.

'I've told you,' she wailed. 'I haven't got four pounds on me.'

Oliver suddenly came to life. 'It's all right, I will pay for Mia, if that's acceptable.'

Sonia gave one of her bark-like laughs. Then she grabbed another four pounds from Oliver.

'Your next tax bill is due in one week's time,' announced Itta. 'Have your money ready, won't you?' She turned to Mia. 'All of you.'

They were about to leave when Mia burst out, 'And I want you to stop leaving horrible messages on my mobile.'

At once Sonia lunged forward and seized Mia by the neck of her jersey. 'How dare you speak to us like that? You ginger-haired nobody.' Her voice cracked with fury. Then she began pulling Mia across the shop.

Poor Mia was gasping for air.

'Let her go at once,' I called, but in a voice so quiet even I could hardly hear it.

Chris Freyer stormed over to Mia. 'Your lack of respect has just caused a tax rise. Next Monday, the tax will be five pounds a week.' Then she murmured to Sonia, 'That's enough – for now.'

Sonia let go of Mia, but so fiercely Mia went sprawling forward like an inexperienced skater, nearly colliding with Oliver. She stood there, gasping for air with an awful rasping sound.

And at that moment I vowed, the day I've learnt karate, the very first thing I will do will be to seek those girls out and terrify the wits out of them . . . and nothing would stop me from doing it. One day I would get revenge for this. But right then I did absolutely nothing. Except watch the three of them swagger towards the door.

Chris Freyer turned round. 'The tax goes up for you two as well. Perhaps you'll teach your girl-friend better manners next time.' She glared again at Mia. 'How's your mum these days? Better, I hope.'

They were about to leave the shop when the

boy's head very slowly bobbed up from behind the counter. 'Excuse me,' he said to Sonia, 'but did you pay for that bar of chocolate?'

'I had it when I came in,' replied Sonia, indignantly.

A total lie. And the boy knew it too. But he gibbered, 'Oh yes, of course. Sorry to have bothered you.'

Enraged now, Sonia stormed down the shop, leant heavily against a shelf full of cans and sent them flying to the ground. 'Ooops!' she shouted.

Then the three of them left, Sonia slamming the door shut behind them.

The boy came out from behind the counter, his neck scalding red. He went over and started picking up the cans. Then half to himself and half to us he muttered, 'You can't win with people like that. So there's no sense in even trying.'

The three of us stumbled outside. Mia started taking deep breaths.

I tapped her gently on the shoulder. 'Are you all right?' I asked.

She just nodded.

Then Oliver announced. 'I think that's our bus.' It was, too.

We scrambled on just before the doors hissed shut. The three of us plodded heavily upstairs and sat on the back seat. I felt so ashamed, I can't tell you. Oliver was hanging his head, too.

'Well, let me thank you,' said Mia. 'You two were great. I especially like the way you both just wimped out and left me . . .'

'I know,' I whispered. 'You've every right to be angry.'

'It's just . . .'

'Yes?' she demanded.

'We had no back-up in the shop. That boy was totally useless, cowering behind the counter like that.'

'I see,' snapped Mia. 'Well, will you just answer me this? Why did you have all that money on you when last night we agreed not to?' She was looking straight at me now.

'Don't know,' I replied miserably. 'I just forgot.'

'You forgot!' she exclaimed.

'No, well, not forgot, exactly.' I struggled to

69

explain. 'I just put it in my pocket as a kind of insurance.' I stopped. I couldn't even explain it to myself. When I slipped the extra money away last night I knew it was cowardly and pathetic. But then I pushed it into the back of my mind and acted as if I hadn't done it.

Mia shook her head. 'I feel really let down by you, Tom.'

'And I feel really let down by me too, if that's any consolation. And I wouldn't blame you if you sat there making chicken noises all the way to school. In fact, I think you should.'

But Mia didn't make any chicken noises, didn't say anything in fact.

We just sat there in this awful silence until Oliver said suddenly, 'I, too, have totally over-estimated my bravery and deserve your censure, Mia.' Then he reached forward and pulled the badge off his blazer.

'I don't deserve to wear this ever again,' he whispered.

CHAPTER NINE
by Tom

That night, in the hut, Oliver told us just why his badge was so special.

At first there was a kind of awkward atmosphere between the three of us. I fully expected Mia to tear into me again. But she didn't. Instead, she said, 'I'm sorry I had a go at you both on the bus this morning.'

'We deserved it,' I said. 'There's no point in saying we'll make a stand and then totally going back on it. We did wimp out.'

'But what did I achieve?' she asked. 'I got the gang mad and we're all going to have to pay them some more money.'

71

'Oh, we're not paying them another penny,' I cried. 'They took me by surprise today. But next Monday I'll be ready for them whatever they do.'

'Perhaps we should wait until your cousin and his mates arrive,' said Mia.

'Go on paying them until then, you mean?' I was surprised.

'Yeah, maybe. Oh, I don't know. I feel all mixed-up at the moment. But one thing I'm sure about.' She turned to Oliver. 'Please put your badge back on.'

She smiled at him.

'And when you said you're not worthy to wear that badge any more, Oliver, what did you mean? You don't have to answer if you don't want to,' she added.

'But it'd be great if you did,' I said.

Oliver looked at us both. 'I'm not supposed to talk about it. But . . .' We leaned forward eagerly.

'This is top hush,' he began. 'And it's to do with my father.' He spoke in this very quiet, unemotional voice. 'He worked for the government. He helped to protect us – he was an undercover agent.'

'Wow!' I exclaimed. 'No, double wow.'

Oliver went on in the same calm way. 'He was supposed to be one of the best agents around. Not that I know all the details about what my father did. But he was one of our country's top agents. I do know that.'

'He makes my dad sound boring,' I cried. 'Want to do a swop?' I was saying stupid things because this was just so amazing. 'Is your dad still a spy?' I asked.

'No,' said Oliver, looking sad. 'When I was five he went away on a very important mission. He found out some really vital information, managed to pass it through, but then there was a bomb in his car . . .'

'Oh no!' cried Mia.

'Was he . . . ?' I asked.

'Yes.' Oliver's unemotional tone slipped for a moment. 'My father was on the trail of a big enemy agent, got too close and they killed him.'

'That's awful,' whispered Mia. 'I'm so sorry, Oliver.'

'After the funeral,' continued Oliver, 'the government gave my mum a certificate and a medal and they gave me this commemorative badge, almost like a medal, really.'

'Oh, wow!' I exclaimed.

'I like to wear it because I think of my dad and feel . . . well he's not very far away. Also, I hope some of his bravery will rub off on me. Not that it did today.'

'Can I have a look at it?' I asked.

'Of course.'

Oliver handed me his medal badge. It was like holding something magic. To think of Oliver, of all people, having this secret life. If the boys in my class knew – well they just wouldn't believe it. They'd labelled Oliver a geek and a boring swot. And that was it.

Until recently, I had too.

But even before tonight I knew there was more to him than that. Much more.

I kept looking at that amazing badge. I couldn't take my eyes off it. And I was so impressed too with the matter-of-fact way in which Oliver had told us. He hadn't been big-headed about it at all.

Then it was Mia's turn to hold the badge. She didn't look at it as long as me, though. Instead, she got up and fastened it onto Oliver's jacket.

'Now it's back where it belongs,' she whispered. 'And I'm really honoured to know the true story behind it.'

'So am I,' I said.

'You're the only people I've ever told,' cried Oliver. 'And the only people I've ever wanted to tell.'

CHAPTER TEN
by Mia

On Saturday morning they woke me up at a quarter past seven.

Their text message was short and not at all sweet.

PAY UP ON MON OR ELSE

After seeing that I couldn't stop shaking. In the end I put the blankets over my head and curled up tightly into a ball.

Oh how I hated their messages. Hated them, hated them, HATED THEM. In fact, I nearly got up and threw my mobile out of the window. Then I stopped myself, because that would have been a daft thing to do — and anyway, they'd just love me to do that.

So instead I lay under my covers worrying about Monday . . . What were we going to do? We'd joked about handing them fake money or giving them the five pounds all in two-pence pieces. But I was pretty certain we'd hand over the money. It seemed the easiest and safest option — for now.

I had just one problem with that. I was flat broke.

I'd insisted on paying Oliver back the four pounds he'd loaned me. And the rest — which wasn't much — I'd spent on sweets and a magazine.

Of course, I could ask Oliver to lend me another five pounds. And I knew he would. But that just seemed to be taking advantage of his good nature. What else could I do? Well, I could always try and explain to the C.I.S. that I only get twelve pounds a month pocket money. And remind them again that my dad was out of work for a year.

It would all just be a waste of my breath, though. Chris Freyer would enjoy seeing me grovel to her. But she wouldn't understand. That chip on her shoulder was so huge it blotted out everything else. So it seemed I had no choice but to put out the begging bowl to my parents.

My dad was home now, but he was not in the

best of moods. I think he was just dead tired with his new job and all the training he'd just done, but he was kind of irritable and impatient. Then, in the afternoon he took my two little brothers swimming: this was the moment to work on my mum.

To butter her up I offered to do the hoovering downstairs. I did it extra thoroughly too.

'That's a big help, thanks love,' said Mum. Then I made us both a cup of tea. She was sitting on the couch, watching the afternoon film, when I brought in a tray of tea and biscuits.

We chatted about this and that, then I said, with what I hoped was a winning smile, 'Guess what, Mum, I'm broke.'

Mum said, 'Oh, really?' in an ominously flat tone.

I pressed on. 'I was wondering if you could possibly lend me five pounds, please.'

'So that's why you've been so helpful this afternoon,' she snapped.

I bristled at that. Mum was right, but she was also being very unfair. I'd helped her loads of times in the past without asking for a penny.

'So what have you done with all your pocket money?' she asked with a sigh. She suddenly sat up. 'Those girls haven't been picking on you again and—?'

'No,' I interrupted hastily. 'And I don't know why

you're giving me the third degree,' I added, indignantly. 'I only want five pounds, that's all.'

Big mistake. Mum immediately launched into a lecture: 'Do you have any idea how difficult things have been for us lately. We've been up to our eyes in debt . . .' Oh, she just went on for ages about how hard things had been. And she ended up saying, 'We haven't got a little money tree at the bottom of the garden, you know.'

Now one thing I hate is when adults say patronizing things like that to you. I was getting really cross now.

'You must try and make your money last,' said Mum.

'Hard to do that when everyone else gets so much more money than me,' I cried.

'Oh, do they really?' answered Mum. 'Well, poor old you.' Then she turned and looked at the television again while I stormed into the kitchen. I gulped down a glass of water and stood by the sink just seething.

How dare Mum talk to me like that. Normally I do make my pocket money last, but the C.I.S. had taken practically all of it this month. And anyway, if Mum had dealt with them properly, instead of shrieking at them in the street and making a right show of herself, well, I wouldn't be in this mess now.

She'd asked me about the C.I.S. several times since. Had they been bothering me at all? Of course I lied. What was the point of telling my mum anything. She was useless. If only I had decent parents who could protect me.

And then I saw it.

Right in the middle of the table was Mum's purse.

It was open too, just as if it were inviting me to peer inside . . . So I did. There were two ten-pound notes and three — no four — five-pound notes. She wouldn't miss one, would she? And I needed it so badly.

So I snatched up a five-pound note, flung the purse back and was crumpling the note down my pocket when I heard Mum.

'Mia.'

I nearly jumped out of my skin. What had Mum seen?

But she came towards me with a big, warm smile on her face. 'Sorry love, been feeling a bit groggy today. Nothing to worry about. The doctor said I'd have days when I felt washed out. It's only to be expected. But I do get so frustrated . . . still it's not fair to take it out on you.' She looked around. 'Ah, there's my purse.' She pulled out a five-pound note. I stared at it, thinking any moment now I would fall through the floor with embarrassment

'Oh, it doesn't matter,' I started.

'Yes it does. I wanted to give you a little extra for all your help anyway.' Then she added confidingly, 'We're not out of the woods yet but we soon should be. And then we'll be able to match whatever pocket money your friends get. All right?'

She put the five pounds right in my hand. So I had to take it. 'Now, don't forget to invite your friends Tom and Oliver round for tea soon. I'm longing to meet them.' On and on she went, being so nice to me until I didn't think I could bear any more. I'd just explode with shame.

But then Dad came back, in a foul mood. He said the twins had been misbehaving when they were swimming and there was to be no television tonight for them. They were protesting loudly about this. And in all the chaos I crept upstairs.

My bed was full of books. I'd thought I might try and sell some as another way to raise money. Well,

I just flung them all onto the floor, then fell on my bed.

I still couldn't believe what I'd just done. I've never stolen in my life before – and to steal from my mum of all people. I was going to slip the five pounds I'd taken back, of course. As well as the five pounds Mum had given me. I didn't want any of it.

But that wasn't the point. If Mum ever found out what I'd done she'd have tremendous difficulty in believing it, as she trusts me completely. I know she does. And she'd say, 'But this isn't like you at all, Mia.'

And it isn't. Only the C.I.S. were bending and twisting my personality into someone who wasn't me.

I remembered suddenly how I'd snatched the money out of Mum's purse just as if I had a right to it. Isn't that exactly how they operate? I was turning into someone just like them.

I paced furiously around my room, then glanced out of my window. It was dark now and practically deserted outside. But I watched one figure walk past our house, go a little further, then walk back again.

It was a girl.

Back and forth she went like a sentry. She wasn't one of the three leaders of the C.I.S. But she was dressed all in black like them. She was obviously one of the wannabes, just bursting to prove herself as a lookout before she graduated to picking on people.

Suddenly she stopped, saw my light. Saw me. And for a moment our eyes met. Then she walked on again. I realized that was part of the plan too. The C.I.S. wanted me to know I was being watched.

All the time they were on at me with their text messages and now this girl . . .

What they hadn't realized is, sometimes you can push people too far.

CHAPTER ELEVEN
by Mia

'So I sneaked the money back to Mum's purse — the five pounds I stole and the five pounds she gave me. I won't have a penny on me on Monday and I don't want either of you to pay for me either.'

It was later that night. I was in the shed with Oliver and Tom. And I'd just told them everything that had happened.

Then I said, 'When we pay them we're putting ourselves in their power. That's what they really love, of course, their power over us. Well, on Monday I'm going to break the spell by letting them know I've no intention of paying them another penny ever again.' I rushed on. 'I know they could batter me. Well if they do, I'm going straight to the police. I'll have proof, won't I. But I don't think they'll do that. They're too sly. And it might be they'll see I'm not as weak as they thought and leave me alone. Anyway, I'm going to try it.'

I stopped. Oliver and Tom had been listening to me in stunned silence.

'You've really thought about this, haven't you?' said Tom, at last.

'Yes, I have. That girl outside my house was like the final straw.'

'You don't want us to pay them either, do you?' asked Tom.

'Oh, that's up to you.'

'I think we should stand together on this one,' said Oliver suddenly.

'So do I,' agreed Tom. 'Together – well we're much stronger.' Then he added, 'And back-up is on its way. I spoke to Mick – you know, my cousin – about coming down with a few of his mates and he's dead keen.'

'So on Monday, we'll all three refuse to pay?' said Oliver.

Tom nodded. 'And I promise you, Mia, we won't have a five-pound note hidden down our socks . . .

no insurance this time. I just wish, though . . .' He paused.

'What?' I asked.

'Well, it'd be great if we could turn the tables on them on Monday, have a little surprise of our own.'

'Such as what?' asked Oliver.

'Oh, I don't know – anyone got a poisonous snake that we could suddenly throw at them?'

'Or how about rotten eggs?' I grinned.

Tom laughed. 'Yeah, that'd be good, firing eggs at them. Or flour. Or . . .' He stopped, then jumped to his feet. 'Set your faces to be amazed. I've just come up with a top idea.'

'Come on, tell us,' I urged.

'Not yet,' he cried, rushing to the door. 'I'll be back faster than soon.'

And he was.

He pulled the shed door open, yelled, 'I'm not paying the C.I.S. another penny.' Then before we knew what was happening he was squirting us both with water.

I spluttered and laughed as I guessed his plan. 'We're going to give the C.I.S. a bit of a soaking, aren't we?'

'We sure are,' grinned Tom, waving the large, blue water pistol about. 'You've got one of these, haven't you?'

'Oh yes.'

'Excellent. So then on Monday the C.I.S. will swagger up demanding money. I'll say, "All right, we'll let you have it." Then we will all open our bags and unleash the water pistols. What do you think?'

I got up. 'I think that in the future when people look up the word genius, they'll see a picture of you.'

Tom liked that. He said again, 'We'll unleash the water pistols.' He liked saying that too. But then we noticed that the third person in the shed wasn't saying a word – just gaping at us in complete horror.

'You're not serious about all this, are you?' he asked.

'Dead serious, aren't we,' replied Tom, looking at me.

'Oh yes,' I agreed. 'I think it's a cracking plan. Our own little ambush and a chance to get our own back for all the things they've done to us.'

'But if we start resorting to violent things like this,' began Oliver, 'we're no better than they are . . . and—'

'Look, what exactly are you beating your gums about?' interrupted Tom. 'We're not committing a crime or anything. Everyone squirts water at people.'

'I don't,' he replied, firmly.

'All right, everyone except you,' said Tom.

I sat down again. 'Oliver, I can understand why you don't like violence. And if my dad had been killed by a bomb – well, I'd feel exactly the same.'

Oliver turned away from me. I wondered if I'd said the right thing, mentioning his dad but he muttered, 'Go on.'

'But after all they've done to us, a bit of water is nothing. No harm's being done to anyone.'

'Of course,' chipped in Tom, 'we could always fire tomato sauce at them. Or glue. Now, what about that?' Then seeing both our faces he went on hastily. 'No, water's just fine. So come on, how about it, Oliver? Are you going to join in the action?'

Tom and I both waited for him to say something. At first he just puffed out his cheeks a bit. Then at last he said, 'I don't happen to own a water pistol at the moment, but I shall be purchasing one tomorrow morning!'

CHAPTER TWELVE
by Tom

He did, too.

A massive multi-coloured one from the newsagents, cost him eight pounds. Then he announced, 'I shall need practice firing one of these.'

So on Sunday night we all practised in the back garden. Oliver was firing too low at first. I told him he must be sure and aim right at the face. Also, we weren't anywhere near fast enough. We had to have split-second timing when we produced those water pistols. And, of course, we all had to be firing at the same time.

We went over and over it. Then we fine-tuned our plan of campaign.

It was pretty simple. I'd say, 'All right, we'll let you have it.' That was the signal to reach into our bags (we'd have to leave most of our school books behind. I thought Oliver might object about this, but surprisingly, he didn't), produce the pistols and then start splattering them.

Each one of us had a target. Chris was mine. Mia was firing at Sonia and Oliver's target was Itta. After we'd finished we had to run like crazy to my house. My step-mum had invited Oliver and Mia round for tea, which was quite handy.

So Monday dawned. On the bus going to school we went over the plan again checking there weren't any flaws. We couldn't find one. We had a final practice on the back field at lunchtime. Oliver was looking a bit shaky now. So, to my surprise, was Mia.

'This is going to be great,' I urged them. 'You'll see.'

On the bus home we checked our water pistols were ready for action. Then, as the bus pulled into the High Street, Mia pointed to a girl hanging around the newsagent's.

'That's the girl who was standing outside my

house on Saturday,' she cried. 'Now she's looking out for us.'

'Don't worry. It's going to be great,' I said, still trying to pump them full of confidence.

'Oh do stop saying that,' Mia cried. 'You've said it's going to be great so often, it's getting on my nerves now.'

'And mine,' chipped in Oliver.

After all I'd done to help them too. Why, I'd turned them overnight into a top fighting force. But I decided they were just very, very nervous, so I let it go.

We got off the bus. The girl I'd spotted had vanished. We began walking down the alleyway.

And then I sniffed. 'That's one thing with the C.I.S. You can smell them three minutes before they arrive,' I said. 'Any minute now,' I added.

Oliver made a kind of gulping noise. I hoped he was going to be all right. Then he tapped his dad's badge.

'Do you mind if I tap it too?' hissed Mia.

In the end all three of us gave it a little tap. Then Oliver whispered, 'All for one and one for all.'

'That's from *The Three Musketeers*, isn't it?' I said.

Before he could reply we heard a clanking, jangling sound and Chris was looming in front of us. 'Got your friends to hold your hand, have you, Tom?' Her voice was mocking and slightly amused.

'That's right,' I replied. 'You never know who you're going to meet.'

The corners of her mouth twitched. She looked at Itta who was standing beside her. Itta permitted herself a tiny smile too.

From the other direction came another voice. 'Well, this is as far as you go until you pay the toll.'

Sonia was barring the way, her arms folded, looking as if she'd gobble up anyone who got in her way.

'Come on,' she shouted, impatiently. 'You know what you have to pay. You should have your money ready.'

This was it. The now-or-never moment. But before I could say the words I'd practised over and over, Oliver said, 'We can't afford to pay you. Could you give us another week, please?'

Mia and I exchanged puzzled glances. What was Oliver doing? He wasn't supposed to be saying anything. I was doing all the talking today.

'A little more time is all we ask, please.' Oliver was looking at Chris really pleadingly.

'We need the money now,' replied Chris. Her eyes were as dead as her voice. Not a flicker of sympathy.

'You can all afford it. So stop messing about,' yelled Sonia from the other direction, sounding impatient and cross.

A shudder ran through me. I wished Oliver hadn't said all that stuff. It wasn't planned and it had thrown me right off balance. I was all psyched up before . . . but I mustn't mess up this time. Oliver and Mia were relying on me. 'Say it now,' I urged myself. And I did.

My voice was perhaps slightly higher-pitched than in rehearsals, but the words rang out clearly enough: 'All right, we'll let you have it.'

Then I grabbed my pistol. My fingers were like jelly, but I took aim at Chris, fired and got her, right in the face.

And I'll tell you, that jet of water was so strong it didn't just drive off all her make-up, but it knocked her earrings right off too. And her hair was soaked through. It was just wonderful to see.

But the most amazing thing was the way that tough, confident mask, which she always wore, just fell off her face in an instant. And all that was left were her eyes, so huge and totally shocked they seemed about to pop out. I'll never forget it.

Mia and Oliver hit their targets too.

Itta was actually bent double and snorting through her nose like a horse, while Sonia just kept moving her head back and forth like a very angry, very confused bull. Oh, how I wished I'd brought my camera. But I knew we couldn't afford to linger.

I was supposed to call out "Go!' and that was our signal to leg it. But I was so high and happy I improvised a little bit here, yelling, 'The C.I.S. are complete spam-heads and can just shove it.'

Mia and Oliver realized that was the new signal to exit fast and we did. Only we couldn't run very fast because we were laughing and talking so much.

We fell into my shed.

'What about that?' I shouted. 'A total massacre.'

'But did you see their faces?' laughed Mia.

'They looked like clowns.'

'They are clowns,' I yelled.

Even Oliver joined in. It was just the most amazing triumph. Suddenly we weren't the victims any more. We were the victors. My head was spinning with excitement for hours afterwards.

Later, I did ask Oliver why he'd gone against our plan and asked the C.I.S. to give us more time to pay.

'I just wanted to try something,' he said, shamefaced. 'Sorry, Tom.'

But in victory I could afford to be generous. 'Well, never mind. The main thing is, our campaign was a total success. We've got them on the run now and they know they won't be getting any more money from us. So come on, a toast to the three of us.' I turned to Oliver. 'Those words you said just before we went into battle. Say them again, now.'

Oliver smiled and looked at both of us.

'All for one and one for all.'

CHAPTER THIRTEEN

CHAPTER FOURTEEN
by Tom

The next few days were very tense.

When Mia told us about that text message we were immediately on full alert. We sat around for hours discussing what the C.I.S. might do, convinced it would be something really bad.

The three of us met up every single night now. And we went round practically all the time in packs of two or three. So now, if I had football training, Mia and Oliver waited for me so that I didn't have to go home on my own.

That was the only good bit about all this: having your mates look out for you.

But each day seemed so long. I kept wishing the C.I.S. would do whatever they were going to do to us and just get it over with. There's nothing worse than waiting for something really nasty to happen, is there? All the time you feel as if you're carrying this great heavy weight around with you.

Especially at night. Then the bad thoughts really crowd in. I'd lie awake, imagining Sonia hatching a really evil plan with Chris and Itta. Gave myself some major nightmares I can tell you.

But one week turned into two and still absolutely nothing happened. A couple of times we had spotted a girl dressed all in black across the road. We hadn't seen her before. But we were pretty certain she was one of the wannabes.

Yet she never looked in our direction, acted as if we weren't there. As for Chris and Sonia and Itta — they'd totally vanished.

Were they hiding somewhere, lying in wait, getting ready to pounce? Or maybe — just maybe — they'd let us think they were going to take revenge on us when, actually, they'd switched on to easier targets? And we weren't in their sights at all?

I hardly dared even whisper that thought to myself at first. But after a few more days went by all three of us were saying it. Perhaps nothing was going to happen after all.

'We can't afford to rest easy yet,' I began, 'but it does seem as if they've given up on us.'

'I suppose there's loads of other people they can pick on,' murmured Mia.

'And ones who'll be much less troublesome than us,' I replied.

Had we actually defeated the C.I.S.? The hope grew and grew. And then something happened to take the C.I.S. temporarily off the front page. We'd had tea at my house and Mia's — but then came an invitation to Oliver's mansion.

Oliver was taking it very seriously, too.

In the shed, he got out a little notebook and asked us, 'So what's your favourite food, then?'

'Mine is definitely soup of the day,' I replied.

Oliver even started to write down 'soup of the day', then he stopped and smiled, 'No, come on. My mum' (yes, he'd actually stopped calling her Mummy) 'wants you to have what you like.'

'OK, tell her to make sure there's lashings of caviare . . .'

'And champagne,' giggled Mia.

'And I'll tell you what my all-time favourite food is, and this is the truth now. Spaghetti hoops on toast. Give me that and I'll be very happy.'

'Oh, I don't think we'll be having that,' said Oliver, anxiously. 'I could ask, though.'

'Don't worry about it,' I laughed. 'I eat anything, me.'

'By the way,' Oliver's voice was suddenly almost inaudible, 'please don't tell my mother that you know about . . .' he touched his badge, 'family secrets.'

'No, of course not,' Mia and I said practically in unison. 'I wouldn't have done so anyway,' I added.

On the day of Oliver's tea party, Mia rang me to ask if I'd be dressing up.

'As what?' I asked.

'You know what I mean.'

'Certainly not,' I replied.

But I did actually select a reasonably clean shirt and gave my comb a bit of exercise.

I'd only seen Oliver's mum from a distance before. I'd imagined her as being very strong and controlling, but instead she spoke very quietly and looked as if she could be in a folk band with her long, dark brown hair and trendy glasses.

Oliver's nan was no taller than me, and sort of anxious-looking (so's Oliver, actually). She kept giving Mia and me shy, little smiles. By her chair was this stick. It reminded me of the night she'd discovered those burglars – and got injured, too.

Before the meal Oliver's mum asked us if we would like to hear some music. I said, 'Yeah, sure.' And then a blushing Oliver sat down at this piano and started playing away.

'Oliver's Grade Four standard already,' hissed his mum to me. I wasn't sure what she meant, but looked impressed anyhow.

Our entertainment over, we all sat down in the dining room to eat (a best china job) and Oliver's mum began firing questions at me. She wanted to know about my hobbies and ambitions, my family. It was a bit like an interview, really, but I suppose that was because she had been married to a secret agent and was used to checking people out.

There were loads of photos about, too, but none of Oliver's dad. I was a bit disappointed about that. I wanted to see if he was how I'd imagined him, but I expect it makes them too sad to see him.

Then Mia got the third degree from Oliver's

mum, while I chatted with his nan. She was wearing these white pearls and to get her into the convo I said her pearls looked dead smart. She burbled away for ages about them. And then when we were all going back into the lounge for a game of Scrabble (!!) I saw her struggling a bit and offered her my arm.

Her face lit up. 'Oh, how kind, thank you dear.'

She leant a small hand on my arm and we were going along nice and slow when she suddenly hissed, 'Do you know, Oliver's mother and myself have been so nervous about tonight.'

'Have you?'

'Well, Oliver's never brought friends home before.'

'Oh, really.' I thought, suddenly, of what a lonely life he must have had, shut up in this house with no friends of his own age.

'His mother and I used to get so frustrated. Why couldn't anyone see Oliver's true worth?' She patted my hand again. 'But now, at last, someone has – and we couldn't be happier about it.'

I was so late back from Oliver's tea party I didn't go into my shed that night. In fact, the next time I went there was the following evening with Oliver and Mia. It was bucketing down with rain, so we raced across the grass chattering away. Oliver was especially high, saying how much his nan and mum had liked meeting us and we must come back soon.

I opened the shed door and straight away an unfamiliar smell hit me. The light switch felt all sticky too. My heart missed a beat. I knew something had happened, but I still wasn't ready for the sight which greeted me when I hit the lights.

Wherever I looked there was this explosion of gruesome, ugly colours. Red, green and purple paint had been plastered over the walls, the ceiling, the windows . . . everywhere.

There was even paint splashed over my work-bench and the sofa. The shelves had all been pulled down and everything on them – all my CDs, books, dripped with garish red paint.

And on the ground, right in the middle of the floor, lay one water pistol.

For a few seconds I was just struck dumb with shock. We all were. I couldn't believe my eyes. I didn't even think they knew about my shed. Then I heard Mia cry, 'Oh no,' very softly.

'They've got their own back, and how,' I muttered.

I grabbed the water pistol and squeezed it. Purple

paint trickled out. I flung it right across the shed.

'I didn't even think they knew about this place,' whispered Mia.

'Neither did I,' I replied. 'They've obviously been watching us in secret.' Just saying those words sent a shudder down my spine. 'And they knew I'd be away last night as they've really taken their time, haven't they, and put so much effort into this.' My voice started to shake.

'Oh, what have we stirred up?' murmured Oliver.

'What did you say?' I demanded.

'I was talking to myself.'

'Well, how come I could hear you then?'

Oliver frowned. 'I never really believed they would just go away and leave us alone.'

'Well, aren't you the clever one,' I replied, sarcastically.

'I knew they'd retaliate after what we did,' continued Oliver. 'All we've done is feed their aggression.'

'I'm glad you said *we*,' I snapped. 'I was beginning to think I was the only one who fired a water pistol at them.'

'I only joined in with the greatest of misgivings,' replied Oliver.

'Oh did you,' I cried. 'What a hero.'

'Look, stop it, both of you,' yelled Mia. We mustn't start fighting amongst ourselves.'

'Oliver started it,' I muttered, 'with all his sighing and acting as if he's above us.'

Oliver turned away. He began prowling around the shed examining all the devastation.

Mia came over and smiled sympathetically at me. 'He's just upset, that's all,' she whispered. 'He's not really blaming you.'

'I think he is,' I whispered back.

Oliver turned round. 'There's a part down here they've missed completely. Not a spot anywhere. Look.' He stood pointing, like an eager tour guide.

I knew he was trying to make amends for what he'd said, but I was still a bit shocked by the way he'd turned on me so quickly. Still, Mia was right – we mustn't start fighting amongst ourselves. So I said, 'Thanks, Oliver, that's good to see.'

He smiled shyly at me. 'We can clean this shed up. We just need a sponge and a bucket of water.'

'We'll do it really thoroughly too,' chipped in Mia.

I gritted my teeth. 'That's right, we can rebuild it, but not tonight. Let's just get out of here.'

For, wherever I looked right now I could see that girl-gang destroying my shed. I could even hear their mocking laughter as they threw paint around.

So we retreated to my bedroom. We sat round on the floor, talking about what colours we would repaint the shed. Until Oliver asked, 'Is that it? Or do you suppose they're planning to do something else to us?'

I shrugged my shoulders.

'I think they will go on doing things to us, maybe even worse things,' he said. 'That's why, to give things a chance to calm down, I'll pay what we owe, pay the whole lot. It's not a problem for me.' Then he repeated the point. 'I'll pay all the money we owe them, myself.'

There was silence for a moment.

'That's really generous of you,' murmured Mia, 'but if we do that, it's like we're giving in to them.' Her voice rose a little. 'And you see, I don't intend ever paying them another penny.'

'Neither do I,' I said, firmly.

'Yes, right, of course,' mumbled Oliver.

I leant forward. 'And we've got to stay together on this one. It's our only chance.'

CHAPTER FIFTEEN
by Mia

The next night we met up in the shed in our grottiest T-shirts and jeans determined to get rid of all that alien paint. We got buckets of water and sponges and slogged away for ages, but – it just couldn't be done.

Then Tom suggested we paint over it. He spun his dad a yarn about wanting to redecorate the shed and his dad obligingly coughed up the price of a tin of blue (non-smelly) paint.

After which the three of us spent another evening of hard labour, and by the end of the night not a trace of the C.I.S. remained. We'd painted them out of the shed.

Tom and I did this really silly victory dance and Oliver tapped his toe to show his support.

There wasn't time to do anything else, but we decided to have a proper celebration the following night. We each arrived laden down with food and drink. Oliver also bought Tom a 'shed-warming rug', and a new cover for the sofa. Tom whispered to me, 'Oliver's just too generous to be true.' Actually, I think Oliver was trying to make up with Tom after their little disagreement.

And we each did our best to be jolly, saying things like, 'The shed looks better now than it did. The C.I.S. has done us a favour, really.' But somehow, it wasn't quite the same atmosphere as before. We were all forcing it a bit.

Then Tom showed us the padlock he'd bought for the door. Now I know he needed one, but it was like a permanent reminder the C.I.S. had been here and might well return. Very depressing.

It was also one of those nights when the wind seemed really noisy. It howled and moaned like the voice of doom out there. And as they'd broken Tom's CD player – and ruined all his CDs – we didn't have any music to drown out the dismal sound effects.

All at once there was a rattle at the door. We jumped to our feet. 'They can't get in,' said Tom, at once. He put a finger up to his mouth and crept to the door. We were certain it was them back again.

Then a voice said, 'We've only come to inspect your marvellous paintwork.'

Tom opened up straight away then, and his dad and step-mum wandered about making admiring noises and marvelling at how quickly we'd done it all. But for a few moments there I'd been really scared. And I couldn't quite shake off that feeling for the rest of the evening.

Next morning we saw Sonia standing in the doorway of the newsagent's. We had to walk right past her to get our sweet supply. She didn't say a word to us – but she had this smile hanging off her lips, and I knew it wasn't just a coincidence that she was there the same time as us.

She was letting us know it wasn't over yet. That attack on the shed was just the first round. By the time we came out of the shop she'd gone, but her little appearance cast a gloom over the whole day. And crouching in the back of my mind was one thought: when will they strike next?

That afternoon I found out.

I walked home with Tom and Oliver as usual. Then I opened the front door to be greeted by a most unusual sound: silence. Usually I can hear my little brothers arguing and screeching. But today, not a sound.

'Anyone home?' I called.

No-one answered.

I peered out of the back window, not really expecting to see anyone there. But I noticed the back door was unlocked. So Mum couldn't have gone far. She'd probably just popped down the road or something.

And then every hair on my head stood up. I could smell perfume. *Their* perfume. I let out a gasp of horror, then quickly told myself I was just imagining it, just as I had in the supermarket a couple of days ago. I'd convinced myself I could smell them. Got really agitated too. But they were nowhere about. That smell only existed in my head. So did this one.

I told myself, 'It's only my imagination,' over and over. I was starting to believe it too when I heard a thud upstairs.

My heart jumped into my mouth. One of them was here. She'd seen my family go out, discovered the back door was unlocked and slipped inside.

I stared up at the ceiling. I was certain the noise had come from my bedroom.

She was up there now. What was she doing? Will there be paint everywhere? Will the whole room be vandalized? She had no right to do that. How dare she . . .

Anger made me brave. I pounded up those stairs, pushed open the door, and saw . . . no-one.

I was quite alone. I also spotted a small pile of books on the floor. So that was the noise I'd heard. I always arrange my favourite books face up (just as if they're in a bookshop, Mum says) and they often fall down.

Of course! Of course!

I could have wept with relief.

I hurriedly put the books back on the shelf. Then

peered round. My room stared back bleakly at me. It felt different in here somehow. Something had happened. Something had changed. I took one more look. My gaze hovered over the dressing-table. Then I felt my stomach squeeze with horror.

My little brown dog – my lucky mascot – wasn't in its usual place in the middle of the dressing-table. It had vanished. But something else was there.

A small, grey water pistol.

I stepped back in total horror.

How long had they been furtively watching my house, waiting for that moment when no-one was about and they could creep into my house, my bedroom? To think of them looking at all my private things . . . I'd opened my mouth to scream when I heard a key turn in the lock.

I sprang to the top of the stairs.

'Mum,' I yelled. 'You left the back door unlocked.'

She stared up at me, smiling. The twins were with her and so was Mrs Adams.

'Oh, did I? Sorry, but we've just been round to Mrs Adams' house for a celebration. Ann's had her baby: a lovely little boy. So we've got a very proud grandmother here.'

'But Mum—' I began. Then I stopped. Mrs Adams wasn't the only one beaming. Her good news seemed to have energized Mum too. For the first time in months she didn't seem drawn and weary. In fact, she looked like her old self again. And more than anything in the world, I wanted my mum to stay like that.

So I forced my face into a smile and said, 'Just leave me a note next time you go out, will you. I was worried.'

CHAPTER SIXTEEN
by Mia

I bolted down my tea and went round Tom's early that night. I had to tell him what had happened. All this pretending to be so happy with my mum and Mrs Adams (she'd stayed for tea) was also giving me a headache.

When I got to Tom's house I started in surprise. A girl dressed all in black was standing across the road. She wasn't one of the wannabes either.

It was Itta.

Just seeing her made my head swim with anger, so I yelled across to her, 'Were you in my house? Were you the one who stole my lucky mascot?'

She stood as still as a statue. And then I noticed her gaze move to a figure standing outside Tom's house. I started in surprise.

'Tom!'

He whirled round and looked really startled to see me.

'Whatever's happened?' I cried.

Tom couldn't speak for a few moments, then he took a deep breath. 'She's been in my garden,' he hissed, at last. 'She laughed at the padlock, said that won't keep them out.' His voice cracked, but then he steadied himself. 'She's still hanging about and I'm so sick of it.' He was trembling. I'd never seen him so upset before.

'Hold on, Tom,' I whispered. 'Don't let them get to you.'

He gripped my hand for a moment. He looked totally shattered.

I called across to Itta. 'Why are you doing all this to us? What harm have we ever done to you?'

Was there a tiny flicker of concern on her face? For a moment I thought I saw something, but then I decided I'd imagined it. She had a heart of concrete, that one.

'Just ignore her,' I whispered to Tom. I put an arm around him. We tottered back to his shed like two old crones. Tom sank down onto the chair. He looked like someone who'd had a really bad nightmare and was still only half-awake. 'Has something happened to you?' he asked.

Moments later Oliver turned up and I told them both about my intruder. They were both really shocked.

'And I've got to go back tonight and sleep in my bedroom,' I said. 'I don't know if I can, not after they've . . .'

'You can always stay with me,' announced Oliver eagerly. 'We've got a spare room. Stay as long as you like too.'

I smiled at his enthusiasm. 'But won't your mum think it a bit odd, me suddenly turning up in the middle of the night?'

'Er, not really,' said Oliver.

I couldn't help smiling. Oliver looked hurt now. 'It's a really kind thought,' I said, 'but I couldn't. And anyway, how could I explain it to my mum? The last thing I want is her knowing about this. And besides, I'm not going to let them push me out of my own bedroom, am I?'

'That's the spirit,' said Tom. 'And we will get your lucky mascot back.'

'Oh, don't bother, it's probably all in bits now,' I murmured, gloomily.

'No,' replied Tom. 'It's what they call a prize of war. They'll still have it.'

'Do you think we should go to the police?' asked Oliver, suddenly.

We both looked at him.

'Breaking into your house, Mia, is a serious offence,' he went on.

'But what's our proof?' asked Tom. 'A water pistol. And if we tell the police they'll be round our houses talking about it with your nan, Oliver – and Mia's mum and dad.'

'Maybe at school tomorrow we could see a teacher quietly,' suggested Oliver.

'But this is all happening outside school,' interrupted Tom.

'They might still help,' persisted Oliver. 'What about Mr Serling, for instance?'

'Oh yes, he's a good teacher, always got time to talk to you as well,' I said.

'But have you seen all the hairs up his nose,' quipped Tom. 'It's like a forest up there.'

I giggled, while Oliver said crossly, 'I fail to see the relevance of that.'

Tom got up quickly. 'Won't be a sec, folks.' But he was gone for ages.

'Do you think we should go and see if he's all right?' I asked Oliver.

'I think perhaps we should,' he replied.

But the door opened and it was as if something of the old, confident Tom had come back. He rubbed his hands eagerly. 'It's all arranged. I'm going up to London with my dad this weekend. I'll see my cousin then and have a council of war. I've just chatted to Mick on the phone too. And the plan is that he and his mates will come down next weekend. We'll discuss tactics when I see him.' He rubbed his hands again.

'How many friends will your cousin be bringing with him?' asked Oliver.

'Oh, a lot,' said Tom, eagerly.

'And what exactly will they all do?' asked Oliver.

'Well, we've got to plan that all out. But basically, they'll be like our secret army, ready to take on the C.I.S.'

Oliver shifted uneasily. 'When we fired those water pistols at them it didn't solve a thing.'

'Yes it did,' cried Tom.

'It just made everything worse,' continued Oliver. 'And if your cousin and his friends start fighting with them . . .' His voice dropped. 'Well, that won't help either. In fact, it will just raise the stakes even higher. And anyway, violence is the language of the illiterate.'

'Is that something else *Mummy* says?' sneered Tom.

Oliver didn't reply, just said quietly, 'I propose we tell Mr Serling.'

All at once Oliver and Tom were staring at me.

'Well, it looks like you've got the casting vote, Mia,' said Tom.

'Oh, great,' I murmured. 'Lucky me.' I considered. 'Actually, I think we should tell Mr Serling,' Oliver let out a huge sigh of relief, 'but only after Tom's cousin and his mates have been here.'

Now Oliver looked really shocked.

'I'm sorry,' I said to him. 'But what can Mr Serling actually do? Not much. While Tom's cousin – well he might be able to crush the C.I.S. once and for all, mightn't he?'

Oliver didn't answer.

'So will you abide by the majority verdict?' asked Tom.

Oliver lowered his head. 'Of course.'

That night I hadn't been home long when Tom rang. 'Just calling to see how you're feeling and stuff.'

'Well, I've opened the window to fumigate the place, otherwise I'm better than I'd expected, really.'

'Ring me any time, day or night,' said Tom, 'and keep chilling.'

A few minutes later Oliver also called to see if I was all right. We chatted for a bit then right out of the blue he said, 'I could still go and see Mr Serling tomorrow, you know.'

'But we agreed we wouldn't.'

'Yes, of course we did. Sorry.'

That was all he said about it, but I was shocked at him even thinking of sneaking off to see Mr Serling without Tom knowing.

The next day Oliver rang to say, 'Sorry I won't be able to join you in the shed tonight.' He said it very casually. Too casually.

He wasn't able to come round the following night either. 'It's nothing,' he said. 'I'm just staying in a bit more.' But when I persisted he said, 'Well actually, my mother thinks I'm spending too much time away from my schoolwork and my piano practice. She also says I'm neglecting my chess and my stamp collection and . . .'

The more he rattled on, the more certain I was that his mum hadn't said anything of the sort. You can just sense it sometimes, can't you. And I did then.

I hated to think that my friend, Oliver, was lying to me.

Even on the bus he was different: not exactly unfriendly, but distant, a bit remote.

And we missed him in the shed. It didn't seem right, Oliver not being there any more.

On Friday night it was just Tom and me. We discussed tactics. Tom was off to London the following morning and was becoming more and more confident. 'We've just got to stick it out for one more week, then victory will be ours. And Oliver will see our way is right.' He gave a half-smile. 'He's sulking, isn't he?'

'I don't know.'

'Yes he is. We're not telling a teacher, doing the sensible thing. Also, he's probably a bit worried that he's their next target. So he's staying close to home. Can't blame him for that.'

'Well, I shall be going round his house to-morrow. I've asked him to help me with my English homework but actually, that's just an excuse to have a proper chat with him. I don't want him slipping away from us.'

'Neither do I,' said Tom. 'Tell him to come round here on Sunday night to hear all the news from my cousin.'

On Saturday afternoon I knocked on Oliver's front door. After a few moments he appeared. His face was very white and he was speaking so faintly I couldn't hear what he was saying, at first.

I leant forward, my heart racing. I just knew it was something about the C.I.S. 'What did you say?'

'They've been here,' he whispered.

'When?'

'This morning . . . they've stolen my badge.'

CHAPTER SEVENTEEN
by Mia

'I still can't believe it,' whispered Oliver.

We were in his conservatory now. 'Tell me exactly what happened?' I asked.

With one eye fixed on the door in case his nan or mum popped back, he began. 'Well, I sometimes do little tasks for Mrs Norman. She's eighty-seven and lives on her own. This morning she wanted some work done in her garden. So I put on my old clothes and left the jacket with my badge hanging over the chair in my bedroom.

'Later, Mum and Nan came round to see Mrs Norman. They'd brought her a plant and stayed to have a cup of tea with her while I came back to do some homework.

'I went upstairs to get changed. My jacket was hanging over the chair just like before but my badge had gone, Mia. At first I thought it had just fallen off. I searched everywhere.' He stared down at his hands. 'Then I chanced to look in one of my jacket pockets and found this.'

He reached into his pocket and brought out one, small water pistol.

'They must have been watching the house, found the conservatory door wasn't locked – Mum and Nan are usually very careful about locking up, but as they were only going up the road for a few minutes . . .'

I nodded sympathetically. 'I'm so sorry,' I cried. 'But at least, well, they can't know the value of your badge.'

'No, I suppose they've just noticed me wearing it and thought . . .' He stopped and hastily stuffed the water pistol down his pocket.

Oliver's nan had popped her head round the door. 'I was going to ask if you wanted any more orange juice and biscuits, but you've hardly started on them yet.'

'Sorry,' I said, smiling at her. 'We've been chatting.'

'Well, I'm only in the kitchen if you need me.'

'Thanks, Nan,' whispered Oliver.

After she left Oliver said, 'The last thing I want is my nan knowing we've had another break-in.'

'But I suppose after a while she and your mum will notice that you're not wearing the badge,' I said, gently.

'I'll just have to say I lost it.' He gazed at his hands again. 'Mum keeps her medal in her bedroom. But you couldn't really wear hers anyway. It's too big. She never liked me wearing mine, thought it was too important to me to wear every day and risk losing it. But I just liked having it with me.'

I was really upset for Oliver. I thought, he's had so much tragedy in his life already, what with his dad being blown up by enemy agents. And now the one thing he's got to remind him of his dad has been stolen.

That's why I said, 'If paying the C.I.S. gets your dad's badge back, go and do it.'

He was really stunned. 'Are you sure?'

Well, I hadn't discussed it with Tom or anything. But I was certain . . .

'Yes, that badge is very, very special to you.'

'So is your lucky mascot.'

'But your badge is more than that. And you can't replace it.'

He got up and stared out of the window. Outside tiny flakes of snow were swirling about madly before sliding down the window and turning into drops of water. He stood watching them, thinking.

Suddenly he turned round. 'No, no. I won't give into them. I won't.'

I was dead impressed.

And for the rest of the day all I could think about was Oliver and his badge. I wanted so badly to do something to help – but what could I do?

It was totally frustrating.

Next morning Mum casually asked me how the English project was coming along. Of course, I'd completely forgotten about that. I also realized that I'd left my exercise book in Oliver's conservatory. I was going to ring him up. Then I thought this would be a good excuse to pop round to see him.

The snow hadn't settled overnight but it was a bitingly cold day and I half-ran to Oliver's house.

His nan answered this time, gazing at me over a chain on the door. Then she opened the door properly.

'Back again,' she said, merrily.

'Yes.'

'And I know why. You left your exercise book behind, didn't you?'

'That's right.'

'Well don't worry, I've put it away in a safe place. So come in dear, and close the door behind you.'

I followed her into the dining room. This was where we'd had tea that day. Now a huge bowl of flowers stood in the centre of the table.

'Is Oliver about?' I asked.

'No, his mother's taken him off to a new exhibition in London. She did tell me which one, but I've forgotten, I'm afraid.' She smiled. 'She thought Oliver was looking a bit peaky and needed a treat. They should be back late this afternoon though.'

She went over to a large, oak bookcase in the corner of the room. At the bottom were two huge drawers. 'Now, Mia, I put your book, for safety, in one of these drawers.'

She crouched down and stared into the first drawer. I looked too. 'No, it's not here, is it?' Then she opened the second drawer. 'Ah, here it is,' she said.

But I barely answered her, and hardly even saw my exercise book. The whole world had become invisible, except for what I'd noticed tucked away in the corner of that first drawer.

Oliver's commemorative badge.

CHAPTER EIGHTEEN
by Mia

It just didn't make sense.

Why was Oliver going round saying he'd been robbed when he hadn't?

There must be a reason. Then I came up with one.

Oliver's badge had fallen off his jacket when he was away helping that old lady, and his mum (or nan) had found it, slipped it into that drawer to keep it safe and then forgot to tell Oliver.

That made perfect sense except for one thing: the water pistol. Oliver's mum might have tidied the medal away, but she'd never have replaced it with a water pistol.

All right. How about this? The gang never actually took the badge — just hid it away? That didn't sound very likely, though. And nowhere near as likely as . . . Oliver faking the whole thing.

But why on earth would he do that? Why? Why?

Because he felt out of things? Because he needed to have something happen to him?

No, Oliver wasn't like that.

There was one other reason. A horrible, terrible reason which buzzed around in my head. I kept swatting it away but it still slunk back leaving a sick feeling in my stomach.

In the end I called Oliver and said, 'I just wondered if your badge had turned up anywhere.' I wanted to give him a chance to get out of this lie with some dignity.

He let out a heavy sigh and then said, in a slow, deliberate voice, 'I'm afraid it hasn't, Mia.'

I was so annoyed by all this pretending that I couldn't speak for a few moments. 'I'm sorry to hear that,' I said, at last. Now I was pretending, too.

He sighed again. 'And I won't be able to come round to the shed tonight.'

'Oh, why not?'

'Mum won't let me, I'm afraid.'

'Oh, go on. Just come round for half an hour.'

'I'm afraid I'm not allowed out for half a second tonight.'

More lies and pretending.

'Give my regards to Tom, won't you. And thank you for calling.' Then he rang off.

I nearly called him back to say, 'Look, I know you're telling a load of porkies. Your badge is in a drawer in your house. I've seen it. So why make up all that total rubbish?'

But then I thought how upset I'd been yesterday. I was practically in tears, in fact. And Oliver sat there, letting me drip sympathy all over him. And all the time he knew his badge hadn't been stolen at all.

I felt a total fool, to be honest. In the end, I didn't ring Oliver again. Instead, I saw Tom and told him everything.

CHAPTER NINETEEN
by Tom

I couldn't believe it when Mia told me that Oliver's badge had been stolen. 'Poor old Oliver,' I cried. 'He must be shattered.'

'He certainly looks shattered,' said Mia. But she had a funny look on her face as she said it.

'How did they know the badge was so special?' I asked. 'Do you reckon there's a mole at our school?'

'No,' she replied firmly. Then she gave the oddest laugh you've ever heard. 'Want to hear something weird?'

'Go on then.'

'Well, get ready, this is really, really weird.'
She gave that peculiar laugh again. 'I went round
to Oliver's house this morning as I'd left my exercise book there. Oliver and his mum were out,
but his nan found it for me. She searched for it
opening all these drawers and in one of them I saw
. . . Oliver's badge.'

I gaped at her. 'But what was it doing in there?'
She smiled. 'Not a lot.'

I grinned too. This was so incredible that it was
all I could do. 'So the gang have returned it,' I
suggested.

'Not according to Oliver. He says it's still missing.'

'Well, maybe there are two badges. Didn't his
mum get a medal too?'

'But hers is different to Oliver's — it's a real
medal — and anyway, she keeps that one in her
bedroom.' She looked at me, then looked away.

I said slowly, 'So you think Oliver has faked the
whole thing?'

'I think so, yes.' She spoke very softly as if she were admitting to doing something wrong herself.

I felt as if all the breath had been knocked out of me.

'Well, I don't know,' I said at last. 'I have a weekend away and look what goes on.' But neither of us could raise the tiniest grin now. I went on. 'So Oliver must have gone out and bought that little water pistol he showed you. He's gone to an awful lot of trouble to trick us, hasn't he?'

'That's what I hate,' muttered Mia. 'The idea of planning it all out. It wasn't just a spur of the moment lie.'

'So why do you think he did it?' I asked.

She shrugged. 'He just wanted us to pay him some attention, didn't want to feel left out.'

'Is that what you really think?'

'Yes.'

'OK.' I hesitated. 'It's just . . .'

'What——?'

'There is another possible reason,' I said.

'Is there?' She said this so sharply I just knew she'd thought of it too, but didn't want to say it aloud. And I lowered my voice a bit before saying, 'Oliver did it so we wouldn't be suspicious of him.'

'How do you mean?' she asked.

'Over the past three or four days the gang have been working on Oliver, thinking he's our richest link.'

'Oh no,' cried Mia, at once.

'I'm just supposing. I'm not saying it's true. But just suppose the gang is leaning on him and he's sort of co-operating . . .'

Mia began shaking her head really fast.

'So to stop us getting suspicious of him, he stages this pretend robbery himself. After all, if he is helping them they won't ever attack him, will they? And one day we might start wondering why we were getting all this hassle and he wasn't getting any.'

'Total rubbish,' cried Mia, glaring at me.

'That idea never occurred to you?'

'No!' she shouted.

'Liar!' I shouted back.

She jumped to her feet. 'I think we're being very disloyal even having this conversation.' She marched to the door. 'I'm going round to Oliver's house now to tell him everything I've told you. Then at least we're giving him a chance and not just making up allegations about him behind his back.'

'All right,' I said, 'if you are totally convinced

Oliver isn't collaborating, go round and see him now.'

'I will.' But she didn't move. Instead, she stood there, shaking her head. Then in a miserable voice she whispered, 'I'm ninety-nine per cent sure.'

'And so am I,' I replied. 'Honestly. It's just . . . well, he has been a bit shifty these past few days, hasn't he? And now this pretend break-in. Something's going on, isn't it?'

'Yes,' she admitted. 'I suppose so.' She sat down again. 'So what do you think we should do?'

'Keep Oliver under observation for a day or two,' I suggested.

'That sounds awful.'

'We'll just do it once or twice, then the whole thing will be cleared up. Isn't that better than having Oliver under suspicion for weeks?'

'So we'll be spying on him,' she murmured.

'Oliver's dad was a kind of spy. You can have good spies too, you know. But don't worry, I'll do it on my own. You don't need to be involved at all.'

'I'm sorry,' cried Mia. 'I still don't like it.'

'So what's the alternative — have a debate about it, witter on for ages . . . ?'

'But he's our friend.'

'And I'm doing it to clear Oliver's name, not to

find him guilty. But he has told us some big fat lies. We've got to find out why. I mean, it might be that he's being leant on by the gang and needs our help.'

'So what will you do, hide in the bushes by his house?'

'Something like that. I'll take some binoculars too and just . . . just lurk about really, and see if I notice anything suspicious.'

'And you don't mind doing this on your own?'

'Not a bit.'

'I'll lend you my mobile, then you can contact me if you see anything. But you won't,' she added quickly. 'I'm certain of that.'

'So am I,' I replied.

She was leaving when I called after her, 'I never told you my news, did I?'

She turned round.

'I saw my cousin and it's all fixed up. Or practically. They'll be here next Saturday.'

'That's great,' said Mia, managing a small smile.

Actually, Mick wasn't completely certain his mates could make it next Saturday. But he didn't think there would be any problems. After all, I was only half an hour away from London by train. And Mick was sure his mates wouldn't want to miss a good punch-up.

No, I hadn't yet told Mick the gang were all girls. I decided I'd brief him about that on the day.

Still, things were definitely moving. And I was chuffed about that. But I'd just been blown away by that news about Oliver.

What was going on?

CHAPTER TWENTY
by Mia

The next few days were truly dreadful. I hated
every minute of them.

First off, Tom said we mustn't let Oliver suspect
anything while he was being investigated (just the
way he said that made my skin prickle) and we had
to act just like normal with him. Well, that was
awful for a start. I felt as if I'd betrayed Oliver
already.

Then, on Monday night, Tom went off to do
stake-out duty (that's what he called it). He hid in
some bush for about three hours with his
binoculars, watching Oliver's house.

Afterwards he rang me: 'Nothing to report, except my back hurts like crazy from being hunched up for so long.' He hadn't seen Oliver go out of the house or noticed any of the girls hanging about.

On Tuesday night there was nothing to report either.

Tom looked shattered the next day. And his back was aching worse than ever. 'Just leave it now,' I urged.

'One more night, then I'll call it a day.'

'You said you were only going to be spying on Oliver for a couple of nights.'

'Tonight is the last time.'

'You want Oliver to be guilty, don't you?' I hissed.

He gave me a filthy look and then just walked away.

Later, that night he called me. 'There's been a development.' He was breathing really fast. 'Can you get down to the High Street?'

'What's happened?'

'Look, it's best you see for yourself. I'm in the phone box just round the corner from the High Street. Get down here as soon as possible.'

My heart began to thump. 'Tom, what's happened?'

'I can't tell you over the phone. It's important you see it for yourself.' Then he rang off.

My dad had just got home from work and Mum was chatting to him. I put my head around the kitchen door. 'I'm going to see Tom, won't be long.'

I'd just opened the front door when Mum hollered, 'Mia.'

I whirled round.

'You can't go out without a coat. It's freezing outside.'

Mum was right about the weather. The cold air hit me as soon as I was outside. The wind was icy tonight. I walked quickly, practically running towards the shops.

But don't think I was impatient to get there. I wasn't. In fact, I dreaded it, as I knew I was going to see something bad.

I reached the phone box. The door swung open. I'd passed it hundreds of times but I'd never been inside it before. It smelt of stale beer and cats. And it was quite cramped with the two of us in there. Especially as Tom was wearing two jumpers and had binoculars round his neck.

There wasn't a glimmer of a smile on his face. And he said in this reciting kind of voice, 'Oliver left his house thirty minutes ago. I followed him. He went across the road to the shops on the left-hand side. He's been there ever since.' He could have been a policeman delivering his report in court. Then he handed me the binoculars.

It took me a moment to focus, but then I had a good view of all the shops on the left-hand side of the High Street: the butcher's, the second-hand clothes shop, the hairdresser's, the newsagent's.

'You'll see him—' began Tom.

'It's all right. I've got him.' Oliver was outside the newsagent's. And he wasn't alone.

Itta was with him.

That was shocking enough. Even though I'd half-expected something like that. What was really shocking though was the way Oliver and Itta were talking and joking together, just as if they were very good friends.

That's what made this encounter so hard to watch. Oliver wasn't only betraying us but enjoying himself while he did it.

I gave the binoculars back to Tom. I wasn't angry, strangely enough. Instead, I felt as if someone had just stuck a pin into me and all the air was pouring out. I slumped against the glass. Tom was looking at me expecting a big reaction.

'I wish I could hear what Oliver's talking about to her,' he said. 'I wonder if he's telling her about us.'

I just frowned.

'I bet he's told her about my cousin as well.'

'Oh shut up about your cousin,' I yelled, suddenly. 'I'm sick of hearing about him.'

Tom backed away indignantly from me. Not that he could back away very far in a phone box.

All my anger and frustration poured out now. 'If your cousin was so great, he'd have come here weeks ago and sorted this out. But he didn't bother. And I don't suppose he'll come this weekend either.'

'You can't blame Mick,' cried Tom, angrily. 'He's trying to help.'

'Is he really?' I said, sarcastically.

'Look, there's no sense us falling out, is there?' replied Tom. 'Then the C.I.S. have definitely won.'

'No, all right,' I agreed. But inside I felt so sick and defeated. Oliver – a true friend, or so I thought – collaborating with the enemy. I wondered how long this fraternization had been going on.

Was it just these past few days? Or had it been longer? Suddenly I had a really awful thought. When the C.I.S. took my mascot I assumed they'd just seen it in the middle of my dressing-table and swiped it. But what if they knew it was very special to me? What if Oliver had told them? No, he'd never do that. And he was so nice to me after the break-in, inviting me to his house and all that.

But maybe that was because he felt guilty. Oh, this was so awful. I felt as if I was being split in two. Part of me staying loyal to Oliver and part of me more and more doubtful about him. Then Tom crashed into my thoughts by hissing, 'They're breaking up. She's walking away and he's crossing the road.'

'Is this where we spring out and yell, "Caught you"?' I said.

Tom gave me a look. 'No, not here. We'll do it properly in the shed tomorrow. We'll confront him there – *and* give him a chance to explain.'

I nodded wearily. Then I watched Oliver walk past us. He seemed deep in thought and never even looked at the phone box. I wondered if he was thinking at all about the two friends he'd betrayed tonight.

When he was safely out of view we scrambled out of the phone box.

'Is that all our spying over for tonight?'

Irritated by my tone, he snapped. 'Look, I'm just as disappointed as you about this. So don't take it out on me, all right.'

Then he gave me back my mobile and offered to walk me home.

'No thanks.'

'Are you sure?'

'Yeah, I'd rather be on my own to tell the truth. I'm going straight upstairs to have a bath. I feel grubby and dirty.'

'But it's better we know, isn't it?'

'Is it really?' I cried. 'I just know I've lost a friend tonight.'

'And so have I. But you're acting as if it's all my fault. You can't blame me for what I've seen.'

'I'm not . . . it's just . . .'

'What?'

'Well, I think you've enjoyed all this spying on Oliver.'

'I did all the hard work, if that's what you mean.'

'When you rang me tonight you were all breathless and excited with what you'd found out.'

Stung now, Tom practically shouted, 'No I wasn't. I had a result but . . . oh forget it.' He started to walk away then yelled out, 'Just remember, you didn't have to tell me about Oliver's badge being stolen. You could have kept that to yourself. You started all this, not me.'

'Thanks so much for that,' I cried. 'Oh, by the way, Tom, I forgot to tell you. I had another message from the C.I.S. tonight.'

He stopped in his tracks. 'So what did they want?'

'They left a question for us: "HAV U HAD ENOUGH YET?"'

CHAPTER TWENTY-ONE
by Tom

The following night, in the shed, Mia was just the mother of all misery. I'm sorry, but she was. She said she'd hardly slept last night, she was so upset about all this. And I believed her. But then she started nagging me about nothing.

'Please stop doing that,' she said.

'What?' I asked.

'Drumming your fingers.'

'I didn't know I was.'

'Well you are and it's very irritating.'

'I'm so sorry.' I clenched my hands into fists. 'You don't mind if I breathe in and out occasionally, do you?'

She didn't answer.

It was nearly seven o'clock and we were anxiously waiting for Oliver. We'd told him there was an urgent meeting tonight and we absolutely needed him to be there. At first he said this wasn't a very convenient night and couldn't we meet tomorrow instead. But I said it had to be tonight.

It had been raining all day and it was just bucketing down now. The rain sounded like hundreds of bullets firing against the glass, while the wind was performing a few special sound effects of its own. Even the weather was expecting the worst tonight.

It wouldn't have been quite so bad if Mia and I had been on friendly terms. But I know she was still smarting about something I'd said last night. I'd reminded her that she was the one who'd started the suspicions about Oliver – not me. I wish I hadn't said it now (even though it was true) but she'd annoyed me with all that stuff about how I'd enjoyed trailing Oliver. Total and complete rubbish.

But I'm the kind of person who, if there's a problem, has to do something about it. A man of action, I suppose. And we had to know what was going on. I mean, it's better to have it all out in the open, isn't it?

Anyway, for some obscure reason, Mia's taking her disappointment in Oliver out on me. So I'm not going to tell her about the fresh evidence against him. It was my cousin, Mick, who discovered it, actually. Got the proof in my pocket. And it's dynamite stuff. I shall confront Oliver with it later.

Suddenly I heard a car outside. Mia and I stiffened. Then someone came sloshing across the grass. The silence in the shed was charged now.

'I hate this so much,' whispered Mia.

'And of course I just love it,' I whispered back.

The shed door creaked open. Oliver stood there, smiling at us both. 'Oh, am I late?' He consulted his watch. 'No, I'm exactly on time. It's you two who are early.' He smiled at us again and sat down on the chair. 'I'm afraid I can only stay for about half an hour. Very sorry about that, but I've got to—'

'That should be long enough,' I interrupted.

I looked across at him, still smiling at us in that absent-minded professor way of his. And I thought, this is probably the last time I'll ever see you here. We may not even speak again, after tonight. In the space of a few days a good mate, who I liked and totally trusted, had changed into someone quite different. And if Mia thought I enjoyed that, then she was barmy.

'We believe you can help us with something,' I began.

Did a little glimmer of fear cross Oliver's face? Had he noticed how strained the atmosphere was? Well his smile had certainly vanished.

'It's about your special badge that was stolen,' I went on. 'Mia knows where it is . . .'

Oliver started, while Mia, who'd been looking at her fingers, now realized I was handing over to her. She swallowed hard. 'Remember when I left behind my English book at your house, Oliver? Well, I went back to get it on Sunday morning. You weren't there but your nan searched for it. And in one of the drawers, I saw your badge.'

Oliver's mouth jumped open with shock. His voice tried to say something but couldn't quite manage it.

I took over. 'So then Mia told me what she'd seen.'

'But why didn't you tell me?' he cried accusingly, gazing at Mia.

'Because . . . because you kept on insisting that it had been stolen,' she whispered.

Oliver's face was paper-white now.

'There's more,' I said.

'I thought there might be,' he whispered.

'All this week I've been trailing you.'

He nodded grimly.

'We had to know why you made up all those lies about your badge being stolen. Last night we found out. I followed you to the shops where you met one of the C.I.S. Mia saw you too. You and this girl seemed to be really good friends. You've been collaborating with them, haven't you?'

'No,' he cried. His eyes widened desperately. 'No.'

I leant forward. 'You faked that burglary so we wouldn't suspect you of being a double-agent, didn't you?'

'No.'

'You're a traitor, aren't you?'

'No, I'm not.'

'At least have the guts to admit it. You are a traitor,' I shouted, really worked up now.

He shot to his feet and made for the door.

'That's it, run away,' I sneered.

'Well, what's the point of staying here, when you've already tried and convicted me,' he shrieked. 'You don't want to hear what I've got to say.'

'Yes we do,' cried Mia, jumping up. She glared at me. 'Give him a chance, Tom.' Then in a much gentler voice. 'Come back, Oliver, please.'

Oliver faced me. 'Do you want to hear my side of it?'

'Yes, yes all right,' I said, calming down. 'Tell us.'

Oliver sat down again. So did Mia. He didn't say anything at first, just sat there with his arms clasped around himself as if he had a nasty pain in his stomach.

'There's no rush,' said Mia, all sweet and gentle. I wouldn't have minded if she'd spoken to me like that earlier tonight.

Finally, in this small, tired voice, Oliver said, 'I wanted it to be a surprise for you.'

I made scoffing noises – just couldn't help it. 'A surprise!'

'Using the water pistols was wrong. And getting Tom's cousin involved . . . well, I knew that would just inflame the whole situation. Everything was getting out of control. And there seemed no way out of it.'

He sighed. 'Then on Saturday morning, just as I told you, I did some gardening for an old lady. My mother and nan also popped over to see her. I came back alone to do some homework and discovered one of the C.I.S. members in my home. I was very angry with Itta: that's the girl I caught. I told her I'd have called the police if it hadn't been for my grandmother.

'Then I explained to Itta exactly what had happened to Nan. She knew there'd been an attempted burglary but didn't know my nan had been hurt or that she's still in considerable pain and can't sleep at night . . . She was very shocked when I told her all the details, and even apologized for breaking in. That's when I realized that she wasn't a bad person.'

'What!' I exclaimed.

'Not completely bad anyhow. And the reason she could do all those horrible things was she didn't see us as real human beings—'

'So you palled up with her,' I interrupted.

'I met up with her again, yes. But don't you see why?' His voice rose shrilly. 'I'd found the chink in the C.I.S.'s armour: Itta's conscience. Now I could use that. But first I needed to gain her trust.

So I had to tread very carefully and encourage her to confide in me. Which she did.'

A little smile of triumph crossed his face. 'She started telling me things. For instance, how she and her step-father get on each other's nerves. She has absolutely no respect for him. Yet she is forced to spend every day in his company. She joined the gang to get away from him.'

'Did she really?' I muttered, and shifted impatiently.

'She also told me that the gang go too far sometimes. She said Chris was always challenging her to do things. And she was getting sick of it. Sonia, she said, was very moody. Some days she'd hate everything and everyone, including Itta.

'That's when my plan took shape. Now, if I could get Itta to leave the gang and renounce everything they stood for – well I'd have split up the C.I.S. and solved the whole problem, wouldn't I?' He stared hopefully at us both.

'But why didn't you tell us all this before?' cried Mia.

'I just didn't think you'd listen,' murmured Oliver.

'You should have given us a chance,' said Mia.

'I know,' whispered Oliver. 'But the way I saw it I had to go undercover, like my dad used to.'

'Your dad,' I repeated, so sharply that Mia looked at me.

'That's right,' replied Oliver. 'So while I was meeting with Itta and negotiations between us were at a precarious state I pretended my badge was stolen . . . just so you wouldn't suspect anything. It was a cheap and silly trick really and I hated deceiving you both. But I think you will agree, it's all been worth it, as something amazing is about to happen.'

'What, exactly?' asked Mia, eagerly.

He turned to her. 'I've told Itta over and over how much your lucky mascot means to you and how nasty it was to take it. Well, Itta has finally agreed to get it back for you.'

'When?' gasped Mia.

'Tonight. Chris and Sonia are going into town to a party and won't be back until very late. So Itta will seize the lucky mascot and then I'm going round her house in . . .' He looked at his watch. 'Oh, in a few minutes, actually, to pick it up. You do believe me, don't you?'

He seemed so sincere, so desperate. But I remembered how he'd told us another tale. The one about his dad and that badge he wore everywhere.

I'd believed him totally then, until earlier this

week when I'd told my cousin, Mick, about Oliver's badge going missing. I described it to Mick and he said he'd seen badges just like that in Covent Garden. I said that was impossible.

But in the post today came the proof. A badge which was a dead ringer for Oliver's commemorative badge. Mick said you can get them for two pounds each (or three for a fiver) on a market stall in Covent Garden.

I had the badge in my pocket and was ready to produce it at any moment. But Oliver seemed so worked-up and upset I held it back — for now.

I decided that if he was telling the truth about everything else I'd ignore the badge. It was a bit sad and all, making out your dad was a hero. But it wasn't a crime.

On the other hand, if Oliver was lying, then I'd let him know I knew about the badge all right.

'Look, just give me a chance,' begged Oliver. 'If I bring Mia's lucky mascot back, then that's proof, isn't it? I know how it looks but you've got to trust me.' His eyes flickered pleadingly from Mia to me and back again.

'Well, how about if we come with you?' suggested Mia. 'Tom and I can hang about a little way from the house.'

'Yes, certainly,' he cried. 'And if you get your mascot back, well, it shows my methods are the right ones – and you'll see why I had to go under-cover and lie to you, won't you?'

'Yes, we will,' said Mia, softly.

A few minutes later we set off. I'd found an umbrella as it was still bucketing down with rain. The three of us walked under it together, in almost total silence until we reached the top of Itta's road.

'You'd better wait here,' said Oliver. 'We're meeting round the corner, outside her house. I won't be long.'

He rushed off.

'I think he's telling the truth,' said Mia. She sounded cross with me. 'In fact, I wish I'd told him all along rather than . . .'

'Than me, you mean?'

'Well, I just hated what you did this week, spy-ing on him and . . .'

'Oh, put a sock in it,' I said, wearily.

'It's perfectly obvious we can trust him, isn't it?' she persisted.

'I don't know. He's lied to us about other things,' I began.

'Like what?'

'Like this.' From out of my pocket I produced the badge.

I handed it to Mia. She caught her breath sharply. 'Where ever did you get this?'

'My cousin bought it in Covent Garden market. It cost him two pounds.'

For a few moments there was silence, save for the traffic swishing past.

'I don't understand,' said Mia, at last. 'Why would Oliver make up that story . . . ?'

'Who knows? I was going to ask him in the shed. But then he was so convincing and got so upset . . . Well, I didn't. And if he has been trying to help us I'll just forget I ever saw this.'

'I really believed his father was a hero,' murmured Mia. She looked devastated.

'So did I. Oh, he fooled me completely. I mean, when you think of it, he spun us a pretty far-fetched yarn, but I swallowed every word of it. He's a very convincing liar, isn't he?'

Mia turned the badge over in her hand. 'Why

would he . . . ? Oh, I don't know what to think now. I'm all confused.'

'So am I. I really hope you get your mascot back, though.'

For the first time that evening Mia smiled at me. 'I do too . . . and not just because the mascot's special but because I just want everything to go back to normal.'

I wanted exactly the same thing. Of course we'd still have the C.I.S. to worry about. But at least the three of us would be together. And if Oliver was telling the truth about his scheme – and I really wanted to believe he was – maybe it might just work too.

And then we saw Oliver coming towards us. His shoulders were hunched and he was walking very slowly, almost shuffling. This didn't look good at all.

'So what happened?' I asked.

He just stood there, head bowed, like a man facing the firing squad. I couldn't help feeling a tiny bit sorry for him.

'Just tell us what went on, Oliver,' I urged.

He looked up, his eyes not quite meeting mine. He still seemed to be searching for words.

'Do you want to sit down?' asked Mia, pointing at the wall. 'You look a bit shaky.'

'No . . . no thank you.' His voice seemed to be

coming from a long way off. 'She didn't have your lucky mascot, Mia, and she's no intention of giving it back either. It turns out she's been playing me for a fool, using me to try and get information. And then one of those wannabes spotted you trailing me, Tom. They thought they'd give you something to get suspicious about. So that's why Itta asked to see me yesterday. It was all a set-up.'

He stopped, gave a kind of strangled sob. 'You do believe me, don't you?'

And I sort of believed him. It's just that Oliver had told us so many made-up stories lately: the fake robbery, his dad's badge. It was really difficult to know what was true any more. I hesitated. I looked across at Mia. She still had that badge in her hand.

All at once Oliver noticed it too. 'What's that?' he cried.

'It's nothing,' she began.

'No, go on, show me,' he demanded, shrilly.

Mia slowly opened up her hand. He saw the badge, gasped, and then stepped back from it as if it were a tarantula or something.

'Where . . . where ever did you get it?' His teeth were chattering and his eyes were suddenly huge and staring. He looked as if he had just seen a ghost.

'My cousin bought it in Covent Garden,' I said. 'Was that where you got it?'

'No,' he cried.

'So where did you get it?' I asked.

'Just tell us the truth now, Oliver,' whispered Mia.

He looked at both of us. 'The truth . . . ' His voice grew louder, more desperate. 'The truth is, I'm not a traitor – I'm your *friend*. Do you believe that?'

Mia and I just gaped at him. And our silence seemed to hit him like a blow. He reeled back from us.

'All right,' he shouted. 'I'll prove it to you.' He started to run off. 'Well, come on, follow me,' he yelled.

CHAPTER TWENTY-TWO
by Mia

Everything became all mixed-up and stupid then, like a nightmare which doesn't make any sense. It all happened so quickly, too.

First of all Oliver raced towards Itta's house and I really thought he was going to march in there and start arguing with her, which would have been bad enough. But instead, Oliver did something far, far worse.

He picked up a stone. And before I could say anything – he moved like lightning – the stone just flew from his hand. And there was a really loud bang as the kitchen window smashed.

I ran forward.

There was just a small hole, about the size of a tennis ball. And the glass around was all frosted and cracked.

'Oh no, what's he done?' groaned Tom in a tiny, scared voice which didn't sound like him at all.

And then Oliver was shouting at Tom and me. 'There, that proves I'm not a traitor, doesn't it!'

'Yes, all right,' I cried. 'Just come away now.' But something seemed to have shattered inside Oliver too. And to be honest, I don't think he even heard me.

Instead, he stood in Itta's garden screaming, 'Violence and fighting, that's the only way to prove I'm on your side, isn't it? Well, there you are!' He shook his fist at the window. 'You've got your proof! Now do you believe I'm your friend?'

Before Tom and I could say anything else, a bald-headed man burst out of Itta's house and started yelling at Oliver in a deep, gravelly voice. A woman with long, blonde hair stumbled out too. And lastly came Itta. She was staring at Oliver, dumb-founded. She didn't say a word. Not that she needed to. That man just went on hollering at Oliver, his face getting redder and redder.

Curtains were twitching all along the road too. One woman with very long hair rushed over. 'I was on my exercise bike in my front bedroom and saw the whole incident. It's that boy over there who threw the stone,' she cried triumphantly, pointing at Oliver. 'I'm a witness. Now, has anyone called the police?'

'I saw one go up the road,' cried some woman in curlers. Then she went dashing off to get him.

Oliver turned and faced Tom and me, his face flushed and drenched in sweat and his eyes wide with horror as it started to dawn on him just what he'd done.

'Do you know this boy?' the bald-headed man demanded of Itta. But Itta just stood there in a complete daze as if unable to move or talk.

The man put his face right up to Oliver's. 'You're nothing but a young hooligan.'

Actually, of all the people in the world, Oliver was the least like a hooligan you could ever find. And he'd never have smashed that window if it hadn't been for Tom and me. Really, we drove him to it, accusing him, never giving him a chance – and then showing him that badge. With a jolt of panic I realized I still had it in my hand.

That man should have been shouting at Tom and me, not Oliver. We'd caused this – and the C.I.S. of course.

I turned to Tom and hissed, 'What are we going to do?'

Tom hissed back, 'Get Oliver away from here as quickly as possible.'

But it was too late.

Moving swiftly towards us came that woman in curlers – accompanied now by a policewoman.

CHAPTER TWENTY-THREE
Tom

I'd never been in a cop shop before.

Wouldn't recommend it.

The policewoman was all right, though. She took down our parents' names and stuff, then brought us tea in paper cups and said we shouldn't have to wait too long.

We were in this deadly quiet room. Mia and I whispered a few words to each other. Oliver just sat shivering in the corner.

The policewoman came back, said Oliver's mum was here and took him off to the interview room.

'Good luck,' I whispered after him. I don't know if he even heard me.

Then Mia's dad appeared. And a few moments later mine, too. They both looked totally stunned at finding us there.

A policeman then came in and said he only wanted to ask Mia and me a few questions. The first one was, 'Is it true that a gang of girls has been intimidating you both for money?'

I looked at Mia, and then said, 'Yes, it's true.'

Next he asked if Itta was in the girl gang and I said 'Yes' again. He said that was 'very helpful', smiled at Mia and me and then said, quietly, 'Those girls aren't untouchable, you know, as they're about to find out.'

Back home the interrogation really started. I think my step-mum realized I'd be better off talking to Dad on my own as she slipped away after a little while.

And actually, that night in the kitchen, I told my dad practically everything. I didn't tell him about Oliver's so-called medal and his pretend burglary — that was just between the three of us. But I didn't try and pretend I'd stayed chilled either. I told him exactly how scared I'd been. And all the time I was trying to read his face and suss out what he was thinking. Was he disappointed in me? Very hard to tell. But he was listening really intently. And I liked that.

When at last I'd finished he said, 'But why didn't you come and tell me all this before?'

'Too embarrassed,' I replied. 'I thought when you heard I'd been picked on by girls you'd think I'd let you down. And I really didn't want to do that.'

Dad looked at me for a long moment. Then he got up and gave me a hug. A real bear hug, in fact. Went on for ages too.

Then he made us another cup of tea and we chatted about some other things. It was past one o'clock but that didn't seem to matter. And right out of the blue Dad asked if I wanted to go fishing.

'You mean right now?' I joked. You see, we used to go fishing quite a lot. But not for a while now, and never since he'd got spliced.

Dad rattled off all these plans for things we

were going to do together. Then I finally staggered upstairs, closed my eyes and five minutes later (or so it seemed) it was time to get up again for school. I thought Dad might have let me off today, but he didn't. Still, at least it was Friday and I was very keen to see Oliver and Mia.

Only, Oliver wasn't there. And Mia and I just chatted briefly. We talked about Oliver, of course.

'We really put him through it. We should have trusted him,' she said, eyeballing me just the way teachers do when you've done something really bad.

'Yeah, you should have done, shouldn't you,' I replied.

We didn't talk again that day. After school I noticed Mia's dad waiting for her. She didn't offer me a lift, though.

I rang Oliver a couple of times over the weekend. His mum answered each time. She was offish and said Oliver was 'too shattered' to speak to me.

'Will you tell him I called and I wish him all the best?' I said.

His mum just went 'Mmm' and rang off.

I also called Mia over the weekend. She'd tried to speak to Oliver too but he wouldn't chat with her either.

On Monday, I came home from school on my own again. Mia had got another lift from her dad and Oliver still wasn't back at school. I was just getting off the bus when I saw Chris and Sonia. They were standing by the laneway I turn into when I go home.

Straight away, my heart began thumping. What should I do? Run away? But they'd only come after me. And they'd enjoy seeing me panicking.

So I walked up to them. Before, when they'd seen me, they'd give me a look of amused contempt as if I were some little worm walking about. Today was totally different. Today they both shot me a look of cold fury. I'll never forget it.

They didn't say a word, though – just went on staring at me as if I were their worst enemy. I began walking down the laneway. I could still feel their eyes burning into the back of my neck. Were they trailing me? I finally plucked up my courage and looked round.

No-one was there.

For a moment I couldn't believe it, then I let out a great sigh of relief because I knew it was all over. Their power over me had been that it was all secret and I'd never told anyone what they'd done. It was a bit like they were blackmailing me, really.

But now my dad knows about them and the police and . . . well, it was a bit like I was wired and alarmed. I've got special protection now.

They could still go on giving me awful looks for a while. But in the end, they'd get sick of that. And they couldn't do anything else to me.

Over and over I said to myself, 'It's ended now.'

Later that night Mia rang me. 'Just thought you should know. I've got my lucky mascot back.'

'What!'

'My mum just found it on the doorstep, propped up against the milk bottles.'

'That's great. I'm dead chuffed for you, Mia.'

Her voice softened. 'Thanks.'

'And do you suppose Itta put it there?'

'She must have. I can't see Sonia or Chris doing it. Oliver said I'd get it back, didn't he?' And again there was that note of rebuke in her voice. I can't tell you how much I resented that.

Then she asked, 'By the way, did your cousin and his mates turn up over the weekend? I forgot to ask you before.'

I started squirming. 'No, they didn't, actually. Mick was let down by a couple of his mates and he had a bit of a cash-flow problem himself . . .'

'I see,' said Mia, flatly.

'Mick did want to help, you know . . .'

She didn't answer.

A few days later at school Mia came up and asked, 'Had any news of Oliver?'

'No, have you?'

She shook her head. And she looked so upset I wished I could say something to cheer her up. But the next thing I knew Mia had just melted away again.

I clenched my teeth in frustration. I mean, it looked as if we really had defeated the C.I.S. So the three of us should have been celebrating together. Instead of which, Mia and I were hardly even talking and Oliver, well, he'd been away for over a week now. And none of the teachers seemed to know anything. What was going on?

I had to see him, especially as . . . well something had happened a couple of weeks before . . . it had been on my mind ever since. I owed it to Oliver to tell him. So in the end I went round to his house. His nan answered the door. In my politest voice I said, 'Oh, hello, could I see Oliver please?'

She looked at me for a moment, then said, quite gently, 'Yes, I'm sure you can. I'll get him for you.' That sounded pretty hopeful.

But I was left waiting there for what seemed like ages. Finally, the door swung open and there was Oliver.

He stood stiffly in the doorway. He looked pale and his face seemed thinner, somehow.

'Hi Oliver, how are you?' I asked.

'Very well, thank you.'

'I'm really sorry about what happened,' I began.

'So am I.'

'Are the police going to charge you?'

'I don't believe so. Itta's family aren't going to press charges and I've already sent them money to get a new pane in the window. So they think I will just get a warning.'

'That's good – not that you're getting a warning,' I added hastily, 'but that it's not worse. Mia got her lucky dog back, by the way.'

'Did she?' For the first time a flicker of a smile crossed his face.

'Yeah, she found it one night on her doorstep, couldn't believe it.'

'I'm very glad for Mia,' said Oliver. Then he added, half under his breath, 'And for Itta.'

I nodded. 'And look, Oliver . . .' I stumbled. It was hard talking to him especially as he'd gone back to being the old Oliver: all locked-up inside himself again. But I had to tell him. 'The thing is . . .'

Oliver's nan suddenly appeared in the doorway. 'Well, don't leave your friend out on the doorstep. Invite him inside.' She smiled shyly at me.

'There's no need, Nan, our conversation is nearly over,' said Oliver.

'Oh.' She sounded disappointed. So was I. She shook her head sadly, then walked away.

I tried again. 'I just wanted to tell you . . .'

He cut me short. 'I have to go now,' he said, firmly.

'Oh right, sure. I'll see you at school then. When are you coming back?'

'I'm not returning to your school.'

That was a massive shock. 'Why not?'

'I'm starting at a new school on Monday.'

'Which one?'

'St Wilfred's.'

'But that's miles and miles away.'

'Yes it is,' he conceded. 'But I told my mother I wanted to make a completely fresh start.'

'And what about . . . ?' I was going to say 'us' but I changed it to 'your friends'.

'I think it's preferable I don't get involved with people too much . . . at my age, school and learning is the most important thing. Nothing must be allowed to interfere with that.'

'Well, I'm sorry to hear you're going to a different school,' I began. It was hard to know what else to say. 'Very, very sorry.'

Oliver stepped back. His hand was shaking now. 'By the way, I'm going to be very busy from now on. So I'd greatly prefer it if you and Mia didn't call on me again.'

Then the door was firmly closed.

CHAPTER TWENTY-FOUR
by Tom

Four whole months have passed since I last stood outside Oliver's house. I haven't seen or spoken to him since that night.

Thought about him, though. And Mia. And all our meetings in the shed.

Of course I still haven't told him what I tried to tell him on his doorstep that night. And he should know. Mia should, too. But especially, Oliver.

Anyway, now I've got to do something. In fact, it's my last chance. As it's the end of term to-morrow and after that . . . well, that's it. I might never see Oliver or Mia again.

So I've written Oliver a note. Here's what it says:

Dear Oliver

I'm just about the last person you ever expected to hear from. But I've got something majorly important to tell you. Can you come round to the shed for seven o'clock tomorrow? I've also invited Mia.

All the best.

Your friend,

Tom

P.S. It really is urgent. So, whatever you think, try and come along.

I posted it through Oliver's letter box. A moment later I heard footsteps and a tiny rustling sound. Someone was picking up my note already. I didn't wait around any longer. Instead, I sped off to Mia's house.

I could have sent her a text message, as the police had brought my mobile back from Chris Freyer's house. But I decided against it. Somehow, text messages still conjured up memories of the C.I.S. for me. And I had a feeling they might for Mia as well. So I sent her a handwritten note too.

I won't bother showing that one to you as it's identical to the one I've written to Oliver.

Anyway after that I went back home and hovered by the phone. I was sure one or both of them would ring, curious to find out more about my mysterious note. But neither of them did. So I sat trying to work out what they were thinking.

My step-mum must have noticed me deep in thought as she chatted to me for a bit. She was really nice actually. But then she can afford to be. She's won.

You don't know the big news, do you? My dad has been 'head-hunted' for a new job in London. He'll earn more money and get a better car, but he's got to move straight away. In fact, they want Dad to start meeting people and stuff before Easter. So while the house is being sold the company is going to pay for us to live in London.

My step-mum can't hide her delight. She's never liked living 'in the sticks'. As for me: well, I still can't get my head round it. Everything's happened so fast.

Next day I said goodbye to my mates at school. They gave me the bumps (I thought you only got the bumps on your birthday – but you get them when you leave as well, or so they told me).

No sign of Mia, though. She's been away all week with flu.

So will she turn up in the shed tonight? I really hope she does but she hasn't rung me or anything.

As for Oliver — I just haven't a clue if he'll appear.

I might be sitting in that shed all by myself tonight.

CHAPTER TWENTY-FIVE
by *Mia*

It was a total surprise.

I was already in bed actually when Tom's note arrived. Mum brought it up. Then she hung about in the doorway while I read it.

'Is there any answer?' she asked at last.

'Why, have you got a carrier pigeon waiting outside?'

She laughed. 'Was it sealed with a loving kiss then?'

I couldn't help blushing. 'Mum, you can be so embarrassing sometimes.'

'But it's part of a mum's job to be embarrassing.

We go on a course for it, you know.'

'I bet you passed with flying colours then.'

She smiled and then sat down on the edge of the bed.

'You won't go until I tell you who it's from, will you?'

Mum folded her arms and grinned. 'That's right.' It was wonderful to see her back to her old self again.

'Well, Mum, it's from Tom. He wants to see me tomorrow night in the shed.'

'About what?'

'He doesn't say, but he said it's urgent and he's asked Oliver to come along too.'

Mum's smile vanished. 'That sounds serious.'

I nodded.

'Do you suppose,' asked Mum, 'it's got something to do with those awful girls?'

'I've been wondering the same thing.'

'Oh dear,' said Mum. 'Poor Tom.'

Yes, Mum knows all about the C.I.S. now.

On the way home that night from the police station I'd told Dad what had happened. He said to leave it to him and it would be best not to bother Mum at the moment.

But Mum soon realized she was being kept out of something and said, 'Only hearing half the tale is getting me more frustrated than if I knew the whole story.'

So after checking again with Dad I told her everything — even how her intervention hadn't really helped. But she was very good about it, said we were going to work out a strategy together. She, Dad and me. And that's exactly what we did. I promised to tell them right away if the C.I.S. approached me again. And then Mum and Dad would decide with me what should be done.

Well, I saw Chris and Sonia a few times hanging about the village and they gave me really evil looks but that was it. And when this policewoman came round last month and asked if the C.I.S. had been bothering me at all I could answer quite honestly, they hadn't.

I still get these awful nightmares about them. I'll suddenly see Chris and Sonia staring through the darkness at me. Then they'll glide closer and closer ... until I wake up in a hot sweat, my heart hammering away. And then I'll put my light on and walk around my bedroom to try and calm myself down. And sometimes I'll think about Oliver's nan and what happened to her. I now know exactly why she still feels scared. When something bad happens you can't just push it away — it hovers over you for weeks, months, afterwards.

I've thought a lot about Oliver, too. Tom told me about the time he'd seen Oliver and how he'd said he didn't want Tom or me to ever call round again.

That really upset me. My mum did offer to have a chat with Oliver's mum, but I made her promise, on my life, that she'd never ever do that. The very last thing I wanted was Oliver seeing me because his mum told him he had to. That would be ghastly.

Mum also said it was a shame I didn't see Tom any more. She also felt I'd been rather hard on him. I secretly agreed with her. But the trouble was, every time I saw Tom, Oliver's shadow seemed to be there too, standing between us. And everything was so tense and mixed-up between Tom and me.

But now there was his message. This looked like an S.O.S. to me. Tom needed help. I'd be dead shocked if the C.I.S. had re-formed, but if Tom was in trouble the least I could do was show support.

So I told Mum I would go round even though I was still getting over the flu. To my great surprise she didn't argue. She fussed a bit: said I should wrap up and not stay too long. And she also made me promise that I'd tell her what Tom said. So I did (and I didn't have my fingers crossed this time either).

Just before seven o'clock Mum drove me to

Tom's house. And I felt so nervous, almost as if I were going to see someone I hardly knew. I opened the back gate. It was still daylight, which seemed a bit weird: every time I'd visited the shed before it had been in darkness.

I knocked on the shed door; I didn't feel I could just barge in after all these months.

Tom opened it, looking both surprised and pleased to see me.

'Hello, how's it going?' he asked.

'Badly, thanks. I'm just bursting with germs, so don't get too close.'

He grinned nervously. 'Thanks a million for coming round.'

'That's OK.' I was really pleased to be back in this shed again, yet I was struggling to think what to say. 'So what have you been up to?' I asked, at last.

'Oh, this and that.' Then a moment later, 'I've started going to karate classes.'

'What's that like?'

'Pretty good. I mean, I've only been to a few. But I'm getting the hang of it.' He grinned nervously at me again.

And then there was a knock on the door.

CHAPTER TWENTY-SIX
by Tom

When Oliver came in I was so incredibly pleased
to see him I couldn't think of a thing to say.

Mia rushed over to Oliver and was about to give
him a hug, I think, but something in his manner
stopped her.

He was standing very stiffly and said, 'Good
evening,' in this really formal voice, frowning at
us both. 'I can't stay very long,' he announced. I
remembered he'd said exactly the same thing the
last time he'd been here, just before his so-called
trial.

'Well, it's great you could make it,' I began.

Oliver gave a little bow, and then perched right

on the edge of his seat. He was wearing his badge, as usual. He saw me noticing that and frowned again.

'Well, there's two things. The first has been on my mind for some time,' I began. 'You know this shed got trashed and we painted it all again. Well, of course you do.' It was so hard saying this aloud. I drew a deep breath. 'Well, just after we'd painted the shed I found Itta prowling about in my garden. I couldn't believe my eyes. She was looking at my shed and laughing.

'She said there was no point in repairing the damage they'd done as they'd only be back to do even worse things to it. And no padlock would keep them out.' I started to speak faster. 'She said there was only one way out of this, to pay the money I owed. She promised she'd keep my secret and then at least my shed would be safe.'

I kind of stopped there for a moment.

'And so you paid them,' prompted Mia, quite gently.

'No, nearly did, though. Itta said she'd be waiting opposite my house. And I had the money. All ready to give to her, too. I was about to cross the road when up you popped, Mia. Much earlier than I'd expected.'

'That was the day my lucky mascot got stolen, wasn't it?' she cried.

'That's right.'

'I thought you seemed really upset that night.'

'Well, you practically caught me in the act of betraying you both. And if you hadn't turned up then . . . well, anyway, you did. We went back to the shed and when I heard they'd been in your house I was really angry. And after that there was no way I'd pay them any money, and that's the honest truth.

'Itta tried again but this time I told her where to get off. But once I very nearly did give in to them. And ever since I've tried to forget about it, bury it away. But the truth is, if anyone was a traitor it was me. And it is very important you both know that, especially you, Oliver, after the way I was flinging accusations at you . . .'

I stopped. My heart began to beat thunderously. I could feel it roaring in my ears. I looked at them both.

'Thanks for telling us,' said Mia, slowly, 'but you didn't need to – and I don't think you're a traitor. It's just that the C.I.S. put you under such pressure.' She looked at Oliver.

'No, you're not a traitor,' said Oliver, firmly.

I let out a grateful sigh of relief. 'I've been wanting to come clean about that for ages. It's been on my mind—'

'And the C.I.S. have been in contact again?' interrupted Oliver. 'That's the second thing you wanted to tell us about, isn't it?'

He said this so forcefully I was taken aback for a moment. 'No, they haven't.'

Oliver looked as if he didn't believe me.

'You can tell us,' said Mia.

I suddenly realized that was why they were here; they thought I was in trouble with the C.I.S. again. And despite all our recent hassles, they'd rallied round to help me tonight.

The mark of true friends.

'Look, I haven't even seen the C.I.S. for weeks. And that's the honest truth.'

Definite murmurs of relief after that.

'No, the second thing I wanted to say is . . .' And then I told them about me moving away on Sunday.

'But it's so sudden,' cried Mia.

'I know – but they want my dad to start right away. Well, like on Monday.'

'Oh, Tom.' And Mia's face went a bit wobbly.

'I'm very sorry to hear all this,' cried Oliver.

'The other thing is,' I said, 'they're going to pull this shed down tomorrow.'

'Why?' demanded Oliver.

'The estate agent's idea. He said it spoils the look of the garden and we'll get a better price if it's not there.'

'That's total rubbish,' said Oliver, outraged. 'You can't let them do it,' he went on. 'Not this shed.'

'But how can Tom stop them?' said Mia.

Oliver sprang up. A wild hope leapt into his eyes.

'Tom, could I buy your shed?'

CHAPTER TWENTY-SEVEN
by Tom

At four o'clock on Sunday afternoon my shed was finally re-housed at the bottom of Oliver's garden.

Dad not only arranged for the shed to be delivered to Oliver's house, but helped a couple of Oliver's neighbours to erect it. And even though it took much longer than we'd expected, Dad never looked at his watch once.

Mia's mum popped round too. And Oliver's mum and nan kept the refreshments going. To be honest, I don't think they were wild about my shed — especially as they already had a very smart-looking sun-house in the garden. But they went along with it.

And it was a great moment when the three of us walked around the shed (which of course I gave to Oliver; no question of him buying it) in its new home.

'There's no electricity yet,' I pointed out.

Oliver waved his hand. 'Oh that's all right, just having it here. Well, I can't stop smiling.'

'We noticed,' I laughed.

'You know,' continued Oliver, excitedly, 'sometimes I'd come back from an evening in this shed and I'd think, I didn't just dream those last few hours, did I? I was really there with friends, a part of something. I can't begin to tell you what it all meant to me. But I was always so afraid it was going to end. That's why I told you both that stupid lie.'

He looked at me. 'Your cousin was right, Tom. You can buy this badge for two pounds in London. That's where I got it.'

'OK,' I said, quietly.

'But when you asked me about the badge I made up something exciting in the hope that it would make me seem a bit more exciting too.'

'So your dad wasn't a secret agent or anything,' said Mia.

'My dad walked out on us shortly after I was born. I've never heard from him since. It was all

190

made up.' He shook his head. 'Afterwards, when you found out the truth about my badge I was deeply ashamed. I thought I'd never be able to face you both again. I just wanted to hide away. I've been very immature, haven't I?'

'Oh very,' I smiled, 'but a great story all the same and I totally believed it.'

'And so did I,' said Mia. 'In a funny way, I still do.'

Then there was a tap on the door and my dad called, 'We've really got to leave now, Tom.'

'The crinklies are getting restless,' I said. 'So I'd better go. Now, don't come and wave me off or anything. Let's say goodbye here instead.'

I turned to Oliver. 'Well, it's all yours now, mate,' I said, shaking him by the hand. 'Look after it for me, won't you?'

'Come back soon and check for yourself,' he replied. 'In fact, it's my birthday next month, April 24th. So we could have my party in the shed. How about that?'

'Great idea,' said Mia.

'And you could stay for the weekend,' went on Oliver, eagerly. 'We've got such a nice spare room, with a really wonderful view of the flower beds.'

'Oh, I'm definitely coming then,' I teased. 'Just to get a peek at those flower beds.'

'And we shall be summoning you to meetings here very regularly,' said Mia. 'No excuses accepted or believed.'

I turned to her. 'See you soon then, Mia.'

We shook hands and then she reached forward and planted a little kiss on my cheek.

'I'll never wash there again,' I grinned. I couldn't say anything else as I had this really bad pain in my throat.

But just as I was leaving I remembered something Oliver had said. It seemed to fit the occasion somehow.

So I turned and said in this croaky whisper,

'All for one and one for all.'

THE END